The Professional Naval Officer

Titles in the Series

Forthcoming

The U.S. Naval Institute
Blue & Gold Professional Library

For more than 100 years, U.S. Navy professionals have counted on specialized books published by the Naval Institute to prepare them for their responsibilities as they advance in their careers and to serve as ready references and refreshers when needed. From the days of coal-fired battleships to the era of unmanned aerial vehicles and laser weaponry, such perennials as *The Bluejacket's Manual* and the *Watch Officer's Guide* have guided generations of Sailors through the complex challenges of naval service. As these books are updated and new ones are added to the list, they will carry the distinctive mark of the Blue and Gold Professional Library series to remind and reassure their users that they have been prepared by naval professionals and meet the exacting standards that Sailors have long expected from the U.S. Naval Institute.

BLUE & GOLD
PROFESSIONAL LIBRARY

The Professional Naval Officer

A Course to Steer By

James A. Winnefeld Sr.

Naval Institute Press
Annapolis, Maryland

Naval Institute Press
291 Wood Road
Annapolis, MD 21402

Library of Congress Cataloging-in-Publication Data
Winnefeld, James A.
    The professional naval officer : a course to steer by / James A. Winnefeld Sr.
        p. cm. — (U.S. Naval Institute blue & gold professional library)
    Includes bibliographical references and index.
    ISBN 1-59114-964-9 (alk. paper)
        1. United States. Navy—Officers' handbooks. 2. United States. Navy—
Promotions. I. Title. II. Series.
V133.W56 2006
359.0023'73—dc22   2005037684

The compass rose design on the cover is used courtesy of the Pacific Northwest
National Laboratory.

Printed in the United States of America on acid-free paper ∞
12 11 10 09 08 07 06   8 7 6 5 4 3 2
First printing

This book is dedicated to a naval legend, Slade Deville Cutter, Captain, United States Navy, retired. A professional, courageous fighter, gentleman, patriot, and friend. His life demonstrated daily that there is more to success in a naval career than promotions. If I could pick only one man to go war with, my choice would be Captain Cutter. If your future shipmates say the same about you, your career will have been a success regardless of promotions, decorations, and plum assignments.

"War is about winning. The best warriors win because they are professionals."
> —From a conversation with Capt. Slade Cutter, USN (Ret.), in December 2004

Contents

Foreword

This book is a wonderful addition to the library of any naval officer, providing wise counsel and instructive sea stories that can be applied at every rung in the career ladder from midshipman to admiral. Rear Adm. Jim Winnefeld, a naval aviator, seagoing commanding officer, former staff member at the Bureau of Naval Personnel, and exceptionally well regarded Commandant of Midshipmen at the Naval Academy, has written a superb volume indeed. Following up on his excellent earlier work in *Career Compass*, he broadens his field of fire from the specific details of career management to the entire ethos of being a professional seagoing officer in the world's finest navy.

Here are a few of the chapter titles:

- What Is Expected of You?
- Leading Sailors
- Transition from Junior to Senior Officer
- Joint and Combined Duty
- Brothers and Sisters in Arms
- Social Polish
- Are You Still Learning?
- Your Command Tour
- Combat: Will You Measure Up?

These are but a selection of the many key topics in *The Professional Naval Officer*, and they are clearly part of what any officer would want to consider as he or she moves along in a career. Admiral Winnefeld's prose is modern, bright, and quite witty. His approach is clear-eyed and never preachy and will age well over time. In short, his advice is simply spot-on.

This is an exceptionally well-done effort, full of timeless advice and a gentlemanly philosophy that will help any officer, at any level, chart an appropriate course through a seagoing career. It is an instant classic.

Vice Adm. James G. Stavridis, USN

Preface

This book is both a complement and a supplement to my earlier book, *Career Compass* (Naval Institute Press, 2005). It is complementary in that there are additional topics not covered in the earlier book and supplementary in that I go into more detail on some topics examined earlier. Hilaire Belloc observed, "There is always something more to be said, and it is always difficult to turn up the splice neatly at the edges." The reader of both books will recognize some enduring common themes: the emphasis on professionalism, solid performance in one's current billet, the importance of qualifying for the most demanding jobs and breaking out of "the pack," and avoiding the seductive lures of easy shortcuts and political maneuvering.

The body of the book is composed of some two and a half dozen essays. Each is a self-contained piece and they can be read in any order. However, the rough organizing principle of the book is oriented to career progression, from midshipman to flag officer. Readers are asked to look back on their careers to date as well as ahead to their future in the Navy.

In this book I am speaking to the reader who is interested in more than the nuts and bolts of succeeding in the Navy and wants to understand the ethos of the service as it is embedded in its promotion, assignment, and professional practices. Consequently there are personal reminiscences (sea stories) to illustrate points learned the hard way in the school of hard knocks at sea and ashore. There is a danger in this more discursive and contemplative approach. Today's Navy is not the Navy I remember so clearly. Mostly today's Navy is much better. The conceit of the book is that there are some enduring truths that apply to naval officers of every generation. This continuity is one of the distinctions and attractions of the naval profession. One of the joys of my retirement is to keep in touch with generations of former midshipmen, many of whom are still on active duty and in some cases have gone on to four-star rank. Living in Annapolis I have ample opportunity to meet and query today's midshipmen, and their instructors and company officers (themselves ten years or less from their own midshipman days). This association across generations of Navy men and women has helped me keep both a long and short perspective of naval officer professionalism and performance. The result is a renewed awareness of the mixture of change and stability that makes the Navy such an exciting career.

I again welcome the reader to join me on a voyage through the sometimes choppy seas of the naval profession. We will note carefully the shoal water that lies alongside our plotted course and the navigational marks that can help us stay out of trouble. You have the conn, but you have a supportive pilot at your shoulder who has shaped his own course through these waters and brought his own ship safely into harbor. Heave in on the anchor chain and let's get under way!

Acknowledgments

Many officers of the naval service have contributed substantially to this book whether they are aware of it or not. My seniors by their example gave me a star to steer by as I navigated through my naval career. That career would not have been possible except for the support I received from my junior shipmates and colleagues. Capt. Slade Cutter once told me, "You know, my crew led me more than I led them. They led me by their expectations of me and I led them by trying to fulfill those expectations." I have been led well in my career by both seniors and juniors.

I particularly want to point out the contributions that midshipmen at the Naval Academy have made to my perspective of naval service, midshipman still in the brigade and others of earlier years who have gone on to high rank.

I owe a special debt of gratitude to Tom Cutler, senior acquisitions editor for the Naval Institute Press. His encouragement and getting an early draft of this book before knowledgeable reviewers made the difference between a published manuscript and a failed one.

Capt. Chris Nichols, USN, reviewed the first draft of this book and blew some of the fresh air of today's fleet through the pages that follow. I treasure his honest criticism, support, and friendship. Cdr. Glen Sears, then serving as a battalion officer at the academy, was most helpful in providing information on today's warfare communities and how "service selection" (really warfare specialty selection) at the academy has been conducted in recent years. Capt. Rich Thayer, then director of professional development at the academy, reviewed my initial table of contents and got me off to a good start by suggesting that I tell the young reader right off "what is expected of him or her in the fleet."

Capt. Tim Wooldridge, USN (Ret.), now plays a key role as a volunteer in organizing the Naval Institute photo archives. Without his able and cheerful assistance in navigating those crowded waters, I could not have put this book together in its present form.

I would be remiss if I did not mention the important role of Vice Adm. James Stavridis in reviewing a later draft of this book. He is one of the preeminent authors of our time on naval subjects. The naval service would be poorer if he had not taken up both the pen and the sword. His suggestions both in this book and its predecessor (*Career Compass*) have made both better than they would have been otherwise. His wife, Laura, also an author, was most helpful in reviewing the appendix on the Navy family.

The book would not have been possible without the steady and professional help of my editors: Linda W. O'Doughda (managing editor of the Naval Institute Press) and Mary Svikhart (freelance copy editor). Together they have helped me understand the publishing enterprise and the effective use of the English language.

The Professional Naval Officer

1

What Is Expected of You?

Now these are the laws of the Navy,
Unwritten and varied they be;
And he that is wise will observe them,
Going down in his ship to the sea.
As the wave rises clear to the hawse pipe,
Washes aft, and is lost in the wake,
So shall ye drop astern, all unheeded,
Such time as the law ye forsake.
—Capt. Ronald Hopwood[1]

You are holding your commission in your hand! You have left the ranks
of midshipmen or cadets behind. Finally, a break from the academic
routine, an end to midshipman or cadet demerits, indoctrination, strict
rules and quick punishment for infractions, and what you probably feel
were unnecessary constraints on your conduct. The real world of the
fleet lies ahead. You are tired of studying leadership and the mechanics
of going to sea. *Now you want to do it!* You feel you are ready. Your officers in your commissioning program have told you that you are ready.
And the speaker at your commissioning ceremony said you are ready.
But what is *really* expected of you when you show up at your first course
of post-commissioning instruction or when you report aboard at the
quarterdeck of your first ship or to the duty officer in your first
squadron? Do your superiors expect more or less of you than before you
received your commission? What do your new shipmates expect of you?

There are many more questions you might ask—including some that may trouble you. Are you ready for prime time?

In this chapter and the two that follow we attempt to answer some of these questions and apprise you of the implications of the major event of your life that commissioning represents. A commissioning is a new beginning. You will find that the habits (good and bad) you have acquired in your pre-commissioning training will follow you into the fleet. While your commissioning is a milestone, it is also part of a continuum. Although you were held to high standards of conduct and performance during your pre-commissioning period, the effect of lapses during that period were for the most part considered a component of the learning process. In the fleet serious lapses now stand a good chance of being made a permanent part of your record. You will at some point be held accountable for them before future promotion and screening boards. Demerits are gone but the consequences of poor performance are not.[2]

Picture yourself sitting in the office or in-port cabin of your first commanding officer. The captain has looked over your record but knows from experience that the record doesn't tell everything about you. You have no fitness reports in that record. Skippers don't know much if anything about your grades in your pre-commissioning program. Even if they did, they wouldn't pay much attention to them unless they were truly extraordinary. You have no professional reputation except among your fellow graduates. Chances are that nobody in the ship or squadron knows anything about you. You have a clean slate, the cleanest slate you have had since infancy.

Your first commanding officer in looking you over sees the raw material that the command must use to create a competent junior officer. They expect that your pre-commissioning education and training has done part of the job, that you have the basic foundation to become an effective officer. You have the academic training that will permit you to understand the technical side of fleet systems and to maintain and operate them effectively. They expect you be in good health and top-notch physical condition. And most importantly they expect you have the fundamental traits of courage, honor, and commitment. They expect that you are self-motivated and don't need to be kicked in the butt to get moving. They also expect that you have left the pranks and games of adolescence behind you (attitudes and actions that a few carry into their twenties or later). Life is no longer a game to avoid being caught by your superiors. You are now a stakeholder in your ship or squadron and you recognize this is serious business. It is no longer what you "can get away with"; it is what you can contribute that counts.

Your skipper expects you to take full responsibility for your actions—for your failures as well as your accomplishments. You will not have to be spoon-fed, given a nanny or a drill sergeant, or chastised for not having the set of personal attributes expected of a junior officer. Your new commanding officer will know that you are "green" and have much to learn. The skipper will forgive much—for a while anyway—for lapses based on inexperience or shaky judgment. But he or she will look carefully for good intentions and a willingness to learn. They will not accept slovenliness of manner particularly when it comes to your duty. There is a difference between "I checked and I misread the gauge" and "I should have checked the gauge, but I blew it off."

Your new commanding officer is asking what kind of shipmate you will be. Will you be a team player or a loner? Will you buckle down—or play around? Are you still blowing off steam after being released from your midshipman or cadet disciplinary regimen, or are you building up a head of steam to help the command do its job? Your captain is looking at your body language and your manner. Are you looking your captain in the eye, alert, answering questions directly and candidly, being respectful but not subservient, demonstrating a controlled sense of enthusiasm, being careful with your language (neither hip-shooting, nor delivering speeches, nor subtle bragging), and so on?

This first interview is important both for your skipper and for you. Each will size the other up. But your skipper has the edge. Skippers have many years of experience at this and are old pros in conducting quick studies. As you will find out soon enough, part of being a good skipper is the ability to size people up quickly and watch them closely (usually without seeming to). Good skippers will probe with great skill and listen to your answers to see what they tell about you. In looking back at my own career I believe my first interview with a new boss was the most important; that interview set the stage for what followed. If you don't interview well, that is a handicap but not an insuperable one. You will have plenty of opportunities to demonstrate your true worth in the months and years that follow your reporting aboard.

There is little you can do to prepare for such interviews, with one possible exception. You probably already know you have weaknesses in interviewing. For example, a tendency to provide lengthy answers to questions that could do with a shorter direct reply, a tendency to let your enthusiasm carry you away, an inclination to try to turn the tables on the interviewer, perhaps a little bit of the smart or hip answer, and so on. Before going to an interview review these shortcomings in your own mind and keep yourself under control. Your skipper is looking for quiet self-confidence that falls well short of smugness, an alert and open demeanor, a person who is serious without being tense or dull, and a person who is at ease in interpersonal interactions. Your skipper is asking: How will this young officer come across to the Sailors in the assigned division? Does this young officer have moral backbone? These and other assessments will be refined over time as you have an opportunity to demonstrate your true worth.

When you leave the office or cabin you want your new skipper to say: "This ensign will do for now, appears to be mature and reliable, seems ready to take up the load, and will probably discharge duties effectively. The jury is still out, but I think I can trust this officer to do the right thing. Looking back on first interviews with officers now on board and perhaps a year or two senior, this officer is above (or below) the average.

First impression is good (or this officer will bear watching until proving his or her ability)."

Mistakes

Every junior officer (and senior officer) makes mistakes. But some mistakes are more important than others are. Of course, as you climb the professional ladder mistakes have greater consequences. Part of being a junior officer is recognizing the stakes involved but not relying on your inexperience to excuse your lapses.

Mistakes fall in one or more of several categories: those of inexperience, narrow-mindedness, poor judgment, hubris, and lapses in moral behavior.

Inexperience
Inexperience is an obvious cause of mistakes. It is your job to get experience, to do so quickly, and benefit from it. You want to shed the "new kid on the block" image as quickly as possible. More importantly you should seek to demonstrate that you are learning and not waiting to be told or spoon-fed, that you are taking personal responsibility for learning the ropes, that you can accept responsibility for your shortcomings. Honesty, curiosity, application, and humility are the essential ingredients of success at this early point in your career.

Narrow-Mindedness
Some mistakes are the result of taking too narrow a view of the problem at hand. In fixing one problem you may generate others—sometimes called the law of unintended consequences. You may think that it is only necessary to get that report "out the door" on time only to find out later that someone reads it and questions its content. Or one of your Sailors comes to you with a problem that you quickly "fix" only to realize later that you have set a terrible precedent for running your

division. You will learn that it is important to know not only *what* is to be done but also *why* it is done. Much of the Navy's work may seem to you to be done "by the numbers" or involve mechanical thinking. From that judgment it is a quick leap to go into automatic. You must acquire the facility of looking beyond the problem at hand and relating it to the whole of your duties—and even your unit's mission. Get the blinders off!

Bad Judgment

Your entire career is spent in a quest for acquiring good judgment. Bad judgment most often results from a lack of hard work in acquiring all the relevant facts, or impetuosity in rushing to quick decisions, or giving rash orders. No book can give you the skill of good judgment; you must acquire it by getting into the habit of logical thinking, setting priorities, doing the spade work of digging out the relevant facts, looking at any problem from more than one perspective, and by close observation of how more experienced officers discharge their duties. Your test is to put it all together in a way that leads to a workable solution, that looks beyond today's problem, and that sets the course for solving future problems. Your boss may give you some slack in the beginning but you rely on his or her generosity at your professional peril.

Hubris

Some mistakes are made simply because officers have too much, but unwarranted, confidence in their own judgment. It is important to know what you don't know—and strive to remedy the deficit. Hubris is an indication of immaturity and perhaps some arrogance. Your bosses will quickly "knock you down a peg" for such behavior. A little humility—but not too much—is in order. Don't fall into the trap of thinking you are smarter than most of the people around you. You will be a poor shipmate and officer.

Lapses in Moral Behavior

You do not have to be told that an officer does not lie, cheat, or steal. If you don't have that basic equipment in your DNA, your naval career will be unpleasant and short. But there is a subset of moral lapses that is more insidious, less obvious, but just as damaging. It includes "gundecking" (falsifying or "editing" reports in the belief it doesn't make any difference or won't be found out), "covering" for a shipmate in a matter of duty or accountability, disloyal behavior toward your superiors, and slipshod performance of your duties (putting personal convenience above your obligations to your unit). Your bosses will be unforgiving in the face of such lapses. You were supposed to learn all this in your pre-commissioning training—and the system *and you* have let your boss down. If you find yourself in such a position, you are in a deep hole and must work your way out with evidence that you have learned from your mistake by demonstrating subsequent superior performance. A few—very few—overcome this handicap.

Summary

To sum up, the Navy gives you a fresh start when you report aboard your first fleet unit, but it is not a nanny and expects you to come up to speed quickly. Much is expected of you in the moral and educational realms but the fleet recognizes it must pick up your training from where your commissioning program and subsequent schooling left off. The fleet's job is to give you experience that builds on your previous training and to test you to see that you have the qualities needed in a professional officer. Things will come at you very fast and there is no room for laziness. A keen sense of situational awareness—relating what is going on around you and your role in it to the big picture—will do much to keep you out of trouble and on a safe course. In striking the balance between watching and observing on the one hand and taking action on the other, lean toward the action mode. Realize that the basis for effective action is keen observation.

While you were at the academy, unit, or in another officer entry program you looked forward to the day when you would receive your commission. You probably focused on the privileges: a bigger paycheck, more personal freedom, and the absence of seemingly petty restrictions and so on. But there is a price tag on those privileges. It is called accountability and responsibility. It is no longer you against the system—you are part of the system. You are now a stakeholder in your command, not a tourist just passing through. Your biggest potential enemy is not the boss who holds you to account. Your biggest potential enemy is you: the temptation to take the shortcut meant for smart people (like you?), placing personal convenience above your duty to your command and to your subordinates, and a failure to push yourself to be the best (not accepting "good enough"). Even if you avoid these traps, the worst mistake you can make is to coast on your previous training (academy grads, take note), or prior fleet experience (former enlisted, take note), or rely on your friends or shipmates to cover for your shortcomings (Mr. or Ms. Popularity, take note). Your commanding officer expects you to have initiative, energy, and an open mind. *Expertise will come in due course but you have to go and get it.* It doesn't just come to you in your bunk or in sunbathing at the pool or beach!

2

Leading Sailors

To deal with men is as fine an art as it is to deal with ships. Both
men and ships live in an unstable element, are subject to subtle
and powerful influences, and want to have their merits
understood rather than their faults found out.
—Joseph Conrad[1]

The basic unit of [Sailors] in the Navy has always been the division.[2]
Depending on the size of the ship or squadron the division may number from three or four Sailors to over a hundred. The division officer
(or a junior division officer, if assigned) is the first commissioned officer in the Sailor's chain of command. When you are a division officer,
you are on the deck plates—and many would say in the "real world" of
going to sea.[3]

Let us assume that you have reported aboard your first ship or
squadron and you have been told that you will be the division officer
or junior division officer for a division containing some thirty-five
Sailors. If you are appointed the junior division officer, it may happen
that your division officer boss is away attending a school. You are in
charge. There seems to be no one about to break you in. As a midshipman or officer candidate your leadership experience has been limited
to leading your fellow aspirants for a commission. Perhaps your only
contact with enlisted men and women has been during a summer
cruise (briefly), or with the sick bay staff during a physical examination, or with personnel specialists prior to detachment, or after report-

ing aboard. You may be tempted (if you have a choice in the matter) to opt for what seems to be a safer job in operations or in some administrative billet and avoid the give and take of leading others. You may argue that you can lead Sailors later after you are more comfortably situated in the command. Wrong thinking! Your best chance of getting the opportunity to exercise deck plates leadership is very early in your career. Seize the day![4]

If you do get a Sailor-leading job right off, it is not surprising that under these circumstances you feel some anxiety. You have textbook learning in leadership but little hands-on experience. Even if you have prior enlisted service, you may have some residual concern. After all, you know the mischievous games some Sailors can play with division officers who are not paying attention. As it is, much is expected of you; but you are short of the savvy that would help you over the inevitable rough spots. You look around and see that some of the petty officers in your division are older than you are—and the division chief petty officer looks downright mature. You observe that things seem to get done without a lot of shouting or the peremptory orders or drama so evident in the films that purport to portray the naval service. You want to demonstrate your leadership and establish yourself in charge, but you are smart enough to know that "coming on strong" and quickly is probably not the best move. Everyone in the division seems to know more about the job at hand than you do. Where do you start?

Getting the Ball Rolling

If you are fortunate and your unit is on the small side, your department head will have time to talk to you and your division chief together. The department head (more commonly known as a "DH") will discuss department policies and priorities with you in the chief's presence and indirectly will remind the division chief his or her proper role in bringing you along. The chief will already know this but your department head is reaffirming objectives and expectations in your and the chief's presence. Your department head will assure you his or her "door is always open" if you have any questions and will tell you not to be afraid to ask them. Questions are better than foolhardy mistakes, and so on.

When you and the chief walk out of your department head's office, a perceptive chief (and almost all are) will suggest that you go together to the division office (if there is one), or work spaces, or chief petty officer (CPO) mess to get acquainted. You have much to go over with the chief. Of that, more later. Inform the chief that you will be looking for opportunities to meet all the Sailors in the division. Avoid group introductions— or making an introductory speech to your division. Sailors hate speeches and lofty pronouncements. Speak to them as a group only when you have something important to say. For now find a place and time where you and the chief can go over the division's manning and get the chief's "take" on strengths and weaknesses if any. This process may have to be spread over several days because your chief is a busy person (or should be). The work of the division must go on and getting you up to speed is an added, though necessary, burden. Make it as light as possible. Some old pros suggest private meetings with each Sailor in order to get to know them. My recommendation is to leave that for later when you have something to say to an individual Sailor, for example, discussing a special request chit, periodic performance marks, or additional school training.

These preliminaries lead up to a most important piece of business. Have the chief accompany you through the division spaces. This tour should be set up so that you and the chief meet the petty officers in charge of each space and major piece of equipment at their shop or workstation. Don't be rushed through this process. Make eye contact with your Sailors and introduce yourself. Some of your questions will come naturally: where are you from, how long have you been aboard, are you married, what are the most frequently encountered problems with the equipment under your care, is it currently operable, who helps you with its maintenance?

Once you get started there will be plenty of questions that will occur to you. In the words of one savvy skipper this is "leadership by walking around." You get to meet your Sailors on their turf where they are infinitely more comfortable. Most Sailors these days are proud of "their stuff." If for some reason they aren't, it is best to know it early. This same old pro also advises taking aboard the fact that, "Sailors were not put on a ship to make *me* look good. *I* was put on the ship to make *them* look good."

You are doing two things in "walking around leadership." First, you are expressing personal interest in the Sailor (learn to repeat his or her name once or twice in your conversation). You are giving the Sailor a chance to size you up—and that is just as important as your sizing them up. Second, you are learning about your spaces and equipment firsthand from the Sailor whose job it is to maintain it or operate it. Those Sailors and the way they do their job are all that is standing between mission success or failure in your unit and don't you forget it. It is vital that the Sailor is informed, motivated, trained, and alert—and you have an important role in each of those four tasks.

All right, you have met your Sailors and you have seen all your spaces and equipment. Now what? The next step is for you to establish, or continue already in place, methods for meeting the division's mission and establishing your relationship with the division chief or leading petty officer. During the time you have been seeing your division's spaces and talking to your Sailors you have had a chance to size up the division chief. Now you need a private meeting with the chief to go over existing division procedures and any suggestions that individual has for needed changes. *Important: Alert the chief right from the beginning that you will have questions and that they are not intended to cast doubt on him or her or on established procedures.* Rather, your questions are a means to assist you in getting up to speed. Avoid a "grilling" atmosphere and above all don't use the occasion to demonstrate your seagoing knowledge or experience if any.

Under ideal circumstances the chief should see you as an asset to the division once you get broken in. You will be able to represent the division up the chain of command and make the chief's assigned tasks easier to accomplish.

Among the most important of your questions is to determine what the chief sees as CPO decisions and what are division officer decisions. How much latitude is the chief given in the administration and operations of the division and what *must* be referred to you? What are the events and reports under the chief's cognizance that require that you be informed? This conversation is vital. Don't be afraid to take notes and pull the string on why a particular practice is accepted. Look on the chief as *your partner* in this dialog, not your opponent or subordinate. When you are done, discuss what you have learned with your department head to see if you and the division chief are on the right track.

More about Getting to Know Your Sailors

You have already met your Sailors but it is time to learn a bit more about them. This should extend to going to the personnel or ship's office and reviewing their service jackets for performance marks, disciplinary entries, special qualifications, schools attended, and so on. Your objective is to become the best informed officer in the ship or squadron on the performance and qualifications of your Sailors. If the command master chief, or the legal/disciplinary officer, or the personnel officer know more about your Sailors than you do, and you don't reverse that knowledge ratio over time, you have work to do.

The Division Chief Petty Officer

We have already discussed how Sailors are your most important resource and the key to effective performance. Now it is time to take a closer look at two individuals who play a vital role in making good things happen in your division: your division chief petty officer and your department head. We will not say much here about your department head except to point out that he or she is your boss, mentor, adviser, and teacher. The department head is not there to hold your hand, accept excuses, or even teach you the basics of the naval profession. He or she has a job to do and you do, too. But it is your job to ease the burden the department head bears. A department head needs workable solutions in even measure with the problems you identify and take up the line.

But early success in your division's performance, fostering the best in your Sailors, and ultimately in your career lies in the relationship you establish with your division chief. With few exceptions these chiefs are professionally competent, savvy, and Sailor-smart. However, in my experience too many division officers leave division matters to their chief and focus on their own watch or flying duties. In short, they see their division officer role as a collateral duty. Often they do this with the best of intentions—not interfering, maintaining the chain of command, encouraging the chief to take charge, backing them up in disciplinary matters, and so on. But don't go into automatic. You need to know almost everything that is going on and you should encourage your chief to keep you informed without getting underfoot or burdening that individual with unreasonable reporting or feedback requirements. Chiefs should see it as to their advantage to keep their division officers well informed. Fully engaged division officers should be seen from the perspective of the CPO mess as a way to head off and solve division problems and to give the chiefs the scope needed to get the division's vital work done.

Your objective is to gain the chief's respect and cooperation—a professional relationship and one you intend to reciprocate. If you see yourself as the beloved leader of children and the chief as their nanny as is so often portrayed in films about the service, you are on the wrong track. Most of the people you see in films or on television have never been in the

The division chief petty officer is the key to that organization's success or failure. Here a CPO is providing hands-on instruction to a crew member.
U.S. Naval Institute Photo Archives

service and haven't a clue as to how things really work on the deck plates. One of the biggest mistakes you can make is to rely on such stereotypes.

The first thing you and your chief must agree on is the primacy of the unit's and the division's mission. Today's division in the fleet is not a rest home, a coffee mess, a waiting station for transfer to the fleet reserve, or a mutual protection society. In the words of one skipper today's fleet division is incredibly vibrant, competitive, and hard charging. The division has a mission and you and your chief need to be clear on what it is and who in the division is contributing and who is not. Candor, humor, trust, and mission orientation should be the watchwords in this relationship—and each represents a two-way street.

The Weak Division Chief

So far, I have painted a comfortable picture: a capable division chief who understands his or her role and yours and is ready to help you climb in the saddle and learn and then do your job. The vast majority of chief petty officers fit this description. But suppose your chief is weak? He or she could be weak technically, or in interpersonal skills, or has simply retired in place without telling anybody. This happened early in my career, and if you are similarly unfortunate you will find that the experience will try your soul. You are confronting early in your Navy life a major leadership challenge. However, first we should observe that things might not be what they seem. A seemingly capable chief may be a "show horse" but is technically a weakling—and you will soon find out that your Sailors know it. Conversely, a seemingly weak chief may just be reserved and quiet but a technical jewel. Your first job is to find out the truth of the matter. There are other anomalies and you must ferret them out, identify them, and if needed set in motion a remedial plan of action.

With a weak chief your first order of business is to hold that individual accountable. To get the chief back in harness and pulling the wagon, he or she needs to understand that accountability for success or failure lies at his or her doorstep. Don't let the weak chief attempt to pass the buck—blaming the supply department, poor Navy technical schooling of your Sailors, poor equipment, having to provide too many extra-detail personnel, and on and on ad nauseam. This situation will

The division chief petty officer is one of the keys to the success of a division officer's success in leading a ship or squadron division.
U.S. Naval Institute Photo Archives

require a variety of techniques to get the chief moving in the right direction. You may need the help of your department head (after all you inherited this chief) and your leading petty officers. But if you work around the weak chief you have in fact written off the key leader in the organization. Don't give up too soon. I would add that you will run into similar problems later in your career—where you must counsel, persuade, and push deficient subordinates to get them back on the team and contributing to the unit's mission. This is one of life's recurring challenges and it won't do to fire or work around the problem; you must solve it.

The chances are that your department head will already be well informed as to your chief's strengths and weaknesses. Your going over division practices and procedures with the department head gives the latter the opportunity (he or she will relish) to put you on the right path and warn you of pitfalls in dealing with the chief or others in your division. Accept this tutorial with an open mind and in good cheer. Better to get it out of the way now rather than later when more will be expected of you. A caution: your department head is not your nursemaid. After a short break-in period you are expected to solve problems and to pass only the most important ones up the line.

If the chief of your division is weak that fact will already be well known in the command and you will find that your division is already receiving extra attention from your department head and the more senior chiefs in the department. The command master chief may also do some coffee-mess butt-kicking with the laggard. But this outside supervision provides you an opportunity to get your chief to join you in running things so that outside interference is not necessary—to together reduce the joint pain level by doing things the way that meets your department head's requirements.

Your Sailors

Today's Sailors as a group are a joy to work with and lead. They are much better than they were in my day. Most old-timers are struck by the difference. Retention rates are high so you keep a lot of your good talent. These rates are so high that they would seem unbelievable to my contemporaries who experienced the societal unrest of the 1960s and 1970s that continued into the early 1980s and rippled through the Navy's ranks both on the mess decks and in the wardroom.

Today's Sailor is motivated to serve thanks to a combination of better pay, better benefits including housing and medical care, newer equipment that is better maintained than in the past, and missions that have a clear relationship to the defense of the United States. Periodic weakness in the economy on "the outside" often reinforces the Sailor's (and his family's) appreciation of the attractiveness of a service career. And

Today's Sailors are among the nation's most dedicated young people, but they still must be led well by the naval professional. Here two Sailors use a piece of electronic test equipment.
Courtesy of USS Theodore Roosevelt; *photo by PHAN Derek Allen*

today's Sailor is better led in my opinion. You have an opportunity to be a part of that improvement.

Moreover, compared to an earlier era today's Sailors are better educated—almost all have a high school diploma, many have gone on to college, and a few have graduated from college. Most have completed an arduous course of technical schooling that in some cases has required more than a year in the training pipeline. You are too close to it to see it clearly, but today's Sailors are sharper looking, trim, and wear their uniforms proudly. Well led they will do anything for you and will be proud of their ship or squadron. They are with rare exceptions drug-free and aware of the problems liquor causes in a family life and in a career. Most have left their racial and gender biases behind them—or have put them aside—and are well ahead of the general population in that regard.

With this good raw material the odds are heavy that you will succeed in your division officer duties. But you are not free of disciplinary or social problems. Your Sailors are young. The average age in your unit may be as low as twenty or less. They have all the impetuosity, susceptibility to making wrong choices, and going with the flow created by their peers as demonstrated by the youth of every generation. You will go with them to captain's mast, you will counsel them, and you will be tempted to become angry with them. What is required from you is patience, firmness, insistence on accountability, and "tough love." A few—very few—will not respond and are better discharged. Fortunately, current recruiting and retention rates permit the Navy to get rid of persistent troublemakers and screwups. But your job is to not give up too easily. The errant Sailor at one time wanted to come into the Navy. It is up to you and your chief to see what went wrong and help the Sailor return to the paths of righteousness.

Many of your young Sailors are married and have started a family. In my conversations with today's generations of division officers and department heads it is apparent that most morale and disciplinary problems are associated with the unexpected demands of family life, the prospect and fact of long separations due to overseas deployments, and making ends meet in a heavily consumer-oriented economy. You will find your counseling duties leading you into situations that you did not expect to encounter. Don't become the "lone ranger" and attempt to resolve all these issues on your own. There are a wide variety of resources available to assist in this work. Find out what they are and use them.

Most commands take special pains to welcome and then indoctrinate Sailors just reporting aboard. It starts with the ship's Web site and personal telephone calls from the command (e.g., senior petty officers in the division or the division officer) to the incoming Sailor, extends to the assignment of a sponsor, and even picking the Sailor up at the airport and providing a suitable welcome on the quarterdeck. This is not coddling, whatever unreconstructed old-timers say. It is good leadership in operation and includes getting newcomers established in their berthing compartments, walking them through their work and watch standing duties, and informing them what it takes to succeed in the new environment. If you and your chief don't see to these seemingly minor chores, you will find that your least successful Sailors will take the new Sailor in hand.

Leading Sailors and Your Performance

This chapter has focused on your duties early in your career and the central role of your Sailors in meeting your unit's mission. We mentioned earlier that you exist for your Sailors, not the other way around. Your early experience in this crucible is one of the major foundations for solid performance over a career of service. If you aren't good (or good enough) with Sailors, you will encounter a rough road in most subsequent department head jobs and in all executive officer and command jobs. Leading Sailors well and being a pro in your warfare specialty are the basic building blocks in your career.

You will return again and again in later years to the lessons learned early on in your service. Few outside your department or unit will know how well or poorly you performed these Sailor-leading duties. But you will know—and if you perform them well, they will become a basis for your self-confidence, professional competence, and pride as you go up the next rung of the career ladder. A hidden benefit is that many of your best Sailor shipmates will in future years become your lifelong friends, a bonus that in my case has carried me into my retirement years. I still hear from some of them forty and fifty years later and see them periodically at ship and squadron reunions. The experience is a treasure beyond measure.

The Division Officer's Ten Commandments

1. If you find yourself giving *direct orders* to Sailors, something is wrong. You should work toward a situation where the giving of direct orders is a rarity and justified most often only in emergencies. Giving such orders is your chief's and petty officers' job. Capt. Frederic John Walker, RN, observed, "A well-led ship's company can be recognized in any emergency by their ready and intelligent anticipation of orders and the absence of confusion and shouting."[5]

2. Just as you expect your Sailors to *meet your standards*, they will expect you to meet theirs. Their standards include fairness and not playing favorites, setting the example in what you demand of them, and orientation to the unit not your own personal benefit.

3. Job one is *getting your chief aboard* (if such is not the case when you take over) and accepting ownership of the unit's and the division's mission.

4. Demonstrate daily that you know (or are progressing rapidly toward knowing) *"your stuff."* You should make it a point to observe closely every major maintenance and operational procedure at least once with your responsible petty officers. This takes time but your progress will be evident to all and you will find that greater mutual respect is the payoff.

5. Keep your *emotions and your speech under control.* Steadiness is the watchword. Better too few words than too many. Avoid lavishness in praise and excesses in criticism.

6. *Beware the Sailor who attempts to end-run the chief* or his or her petty officers. Your first question should be: Who is your leading petty officer and does he or she know this? If not, why not? Don't accept quibbles or excuses in their answers.

7. Insist on *accountability.* There is a chain of accountability in your division from top to bottom. Someone is to blame or to be credited

when things go wrong or right. Good intentions are never a sufficient explanation. Find the source of the problem and then fix it.

8. *Avoid a myopic focus on your own job.* Look up to your department
   head and out to other divisions and departments to see how all the
   pieces fit. This is not only the pathway to professional growth but
   also will help you keep the work of your division in perspective.
   Seeing the big picture means seeing the forest *and* the trees at the
   same time.

9. *Loyalty is a two-way street.* Just as you must earn the respect of your
   Sailors, they must earn yours by their performance. When you back
   up your Sailors it is a token of respect that they have earned whether
   it is for a good performance evaluation or a recommendation for
   leniency at mast.

10. The *example* you set is important. Your uniform, your demeanor,
    your focus on the unit's mission, and your diligence set the tone for
    your division. Your Sailors, in ways you will not understand, will
    watch your every move and will be the first to detect a false note.

We began this chapter with a quote from Joseph Conrad and so we shall
end it. "It is the captain who puts the ship ashore; it is *we* who got her
off."[6] Your good judgment and your bluejackets are all that stand
between you and failure.

3

Operational Performance

> The attainment of proficiency, the pushing of your skill with attention to the most delicate shades of excellence, is a matter of vital concern [to the seaman].
> —Joseph Conrad[1]

Leading Sailors is block one, and operating and maintaining your warfare platform (including all major systems in your ship or squadron) is block two on the road to professional competence as a junior officer. Because there are so many such systems, in this chapter we must rely mainly on broad strokes and use specifics only to illustrate a point. There is little obvious similarity between being diving officer on a submarine, being the pilot of an attack aircraft, being the officer of the deck of a destroyer going alongside an oiler, or being a nuclear reactor watch officer deep in the bowels of an aircraft carrier. But one of the common strands that links this band of brothers and sisters is that they have passed the test and have become pros.

When you arrive on board you will regard with respect and perhaps some awe those officers who are two or more years ahead of you in this learning process. They will be the patrol plane commanders, the officers of the deck, the fully qualified engineers. While some of you may wear wings you will be only too aware that you have not qualified in the school that counts. Despite the good job the fleet replacement squadron does, it is only a point of departure for the full carrier and weapons qualifications that define the true pro. If you are an embryonic surface warfare or submarine officer, you will look forward to winning your surface warfare pin or dolphins. The holy grail for many is to be designated an officer of the deck under way and to earn the skipper's confidence to entrust his or her ship to your care. Of commensurate importance is gaining your engineering officer of the watch qualification.

You will soon learn that becoming operationally proficient depends on securing a large number of qualifications in sequence. Your first job is to find out what these qualifications are and to lay out a program for achieving them. You will get a great deal of help in this endeavor. There are detailed and complex training and qualification programs to guide you along the way. After finding out what the ladder upward looks like your next job is to take ownership of the challenge presented. You must be proactive in managing your own career while using the help available. Do not take a hands-off approach to getting qualified. Your objective is to learn the profession and to do so as quickly as thoroughness permits. Don't be the last in your crop to get the designation you seek. You should start and end your career in a full-speed sprint and wanting to be first.

Being first or second requires a great deal of intensive study and application. It doesn't just come to you when it is your turn. Your seniors will be quick to see your diligence and application, and they will lend a helping hand. Let us use the officer of the deck under way qualification as an example. Let me add that even you (we) aviators can benefit by listening up. If you stay in the service, the odds are heavy that there are ship's company duties in your future. The techniques cited below apply to you even if the subject matter is in a different warfare specialty.

The Officer of the Deck Under Way

In the centuries predating the awarding of the surface warfare qualification and pin, the officer of the deck (OOD) under way designation was the most sought and a tangible demonstration that a young officer had arrived. The junior officer had learned the basics of watch keeping, conning a ship, and gaining the skipper's confidence. The qualification was a testimonial to the officer's good judgment, diligent study, and reliability. Today the qualification is still important but as a major milestone on the road to earning dolphins or a surface warfare pin.

The syllabus leading to qualification today is extensive, intensive, and rigorous. Everyone doesn't succeed. In my day qualification was more informal and much of it was seat of the pants: you either had the skipper's confidence or you did not. The book learning aspect was a "given." One would start by being a "bridge rat" standing junior officer of the deck watches, "punching" the tactical publications, taking routine reports from other watch standers, becoming familiar with the equipment on the bridge (today more complex than ever), and performing the routine tasks of rudimentary station keeping, and so on. There were drills and exercises to be performed and mastered (e.g., man overboard, general quarters, sea detail) and exams to be taken (e.g., rules of the nautical road, tactical maneuvering, engineering plant familiarization) but in the last analysis it came down to the senior watch officer's judgment that you were ready to become an OOD and recommending such to the skipper.

The first step was to become OOD during daylight with the ship steaming independently. Then might come independent steaming at night, then might come OOD under way in formation during the daytime, and finally OOD in formation at night. This was the final set of laurels and signaled that the captain felt comfortable (or almost so) in turning in to the bunk in the sea cabin while you were not only master of your fate but also of some hundreds of other shipmates as well. As an aviator I can say I never felt such pride and a load of responsibility as when I qualified as OOD at night in a destroyer in Korean waters in the early 1950s. Looking back on the event, it was a defining moment in my career, and I will bet a similar qualification will be in yours as well.

Today the process is much more structured and the testing more rigorous. You are given ample opportunities to conn the ship, exercise at

It is in any officer's best interest to become qualified for demanding jobs as soon as thoroughness permits. The officer of the deck of USS *George Washington* (CVN-73) shown here has the advantage of coming under the daily observation of his skipper (seated).
U.S. Naval Institute Photo Archives

drills, and experience the anxiety of taking examinations. The critical exams are oral and conducted at two levels: the first is usually chaired by the senior watch officer (or the senior department head) and the second is chaired by the skipper. The first is a screening board and in well-run ships is tougher than the second where the skipper relies heavily on the earlier screening. A few years back I had the opportunity to sit in on two such oral examinations as an observer. The scope and depth of the questioning—and the knowledge demonstrated by the test-takers—were impressive. One candidate passed and one was given three months to prepare to take the exam again. The examiners gave nothing away; the test taker had to earn the board's confidence. After the officer left the cabin, the board went over the candidate's answers in detail probing for weakness, signs of initiative and situational awareness, and whether or not the individual was ready.

A couple of things should stand out from this tour of the way things were and the way things are today. First, you are the central player. No one is going to spoon-feed this stuff into you. You must want the qualification and you must work hard to get it. Second, while book learning and rote memorization are needed, they are not sufficient. You may have been a good test taker in high school or college, but watch standing examinations probe the whole person. Do you panic? Are you shaky once you leave the pat problems and solutions offered by the textbooks? Are you thinking or are you memorizing? Are you decisive or hesitant? Do you have the courage to admit to others that you don't know the answer to a question—but then go on and demonstrate the diligence to find it? Finally, when you parse problems and arrive at a solution, do you demonstrate good judgment?

Other qualifications and warfare specialties also rely on the oral examination capstone of the qualification process. The good news is that you can systematically prepare for them. You will find that there is wardroom or ready room lore of frequently asked questions. Some units may even have them written down as tuning-up exercises. Moreover, some of the same questions may be asked in your bouts with the boards—just to see if you are paying attention.

But the most important step you can take is to prepare *your own questions* based on the subject matter of the exam. Don't limit yourself to the questions for which you have the answer. Stretch the envelope and ask questions that you believe should or might be asked. Then formulate the answers—not shooting from the hip or memory—but from the key references. *Write them down.* It takes time, but the effort has a quadruple payoff: you will have a better grasp of the subject matter, you will have a ready reference for further review, you will have a basis for getting others to go over the material with you, and you will improve your clarity and completeness in writing.

To continue this discussion of preparation, do you know of items that the skipper is particularly interested in? Or of special interest to the department heads who are sitting as board members? For example, you can bet the chief engineer will test your knowledge of the plant, and those in charge of combat systems will ask you about such things as weapons release authority. Expect the skipper to quiz you closely on his or her standing night orders. Corresponding boards for aviation units will be keenly interested in your understanding of Naval Air Training and Operating Procedures Standardization (NATOPS, aircraft operating procedures), in-flight emergencies, rules of engagement, and flight discipline in formation or around the carrier.

Your Report Card

Your progress in getting over the many hurdles in becoming a pro will find its way into your fitness reports. Not just that you got over a particular hurdle but also the diligence and class you demonstrated in doing it. These qualification hurdles offer you prime "face time" with the people that run your unit and an opportunity to demonstrate to them that you know your stuff. In a large ship or squadron this may be one of the few times you get to converse on a professional subject with your skipper. The captain is sizing you up in other dimensions not limited to the subject matter of the examination. If you do well, the benefits can come back to you in the form of more responsible jobs (yes, the Navy still does fleet up), getting qualified for the next rung on the ladder, and last but not least, a good fitness report.

When you leave your first ship or squadron, you should be able to look back on a tour that turned you into a pro—proficient in leading Sailors, with expertise in operating and maintaining your weapons platform, and the sound judgment that is so eagerly sought when the Navy picks its future department heads and skippers. I can guarantee you that this experience will carry you through a Navy career. It comprises a resource that you will draw on time after time as you rise to be a skipper yourself and perhaps to flag rank as well.

Let me close with a sea story from my own personal experience that illustrates the points I have made. As already mentioned I qualified as an OOD of a destroyer during the Korean War. Later in my first squadron flying from a carrier, a squadron mate of mine and I had an opportunity to get qualified as OODs of our carrier. At the time we considered it a novelty and that our qualification would be pro forma. (What does the air group know about driving a ship?) But the skeptics reckoned not with the carrier skipper's interest in this experiment. After getting our squadron skipper's agreement, we were qualified and slipped into a one in six or eight rotation as fully qualified carrier OODs in formation—much to the chagrin of the officer in charge of drawing up our squadron's flight schedule. I recall one evening after a twilight recovery of my squadron that I had to rush to my stateroom, change out of flight gear, grab a quick sandwich, and report to the bridge to relieve the watch as OOD for the evening watch. This was an epiphany for me: suddenly the component parts of a naval officer's business clicked into place with a clang that rings in my ears until this day.

But the story does not end there. More than ten years later, I was the executive officer of an embarked squadron in a carrier in the Tonkin Gulf. Several of us with some sea experience were recruited to stand command duty officer (CDO) watches on the bridge during night air operations. Because our carrier was conducting around-the-clock air operations, the CDO watch stander gave the skipper a chance to get some much-needed rest. While standing these watches I had to reach deep into my previous tours as OOD to exercise the judgment the occasion called for. In one case our FOXTROT CORPEN (aircraft recovery course) took us directly toward the coast of North Vietnam some thirty-five miles away. Add to that an aircraft in the landing pattern with insufficient fuel to bingo (go to a divert field) and having trouble getting aboard.

There are further chapters to this story but let us leave it here and say that you will find as I did that those early days at sea are critical to your success as a naval officer—success in getting your unit's job done. Block by block you are building the edifice of professional competence. You skip or glide over a step at your professional peril.

4

Performance in the Schoolhouse

What is your *principal* motive for pursuing a postgraduate
course of instruction? To be a better sea officer? To be a better
officer in shore billets? To get ready for a civilian career? To
add to your resume? For the intellectual challenge? To prepare
for possible transfer to the restricted line or staff corps?
Ordering these questions in some sort of priority and being
brutally honest with yourself will tell you a great deal about
your true priorities.
—Rear Adm. James A. Winnefeld[1]

You have finished your first tours of sea duty and are headed ashore.
The odds are high that you will go ashore to one of the Navy's numerous schoolhouses. You will go either as a student, an instructor, or as a
member of the support staff. There are benefits associated with each
path. Many of you will be ready for adventures of the mind after an
arduous sea tour punctuated by deployments, high operations tempo,
frequent inspections and exercises, and perhaps the added spice of service in a combat zone. As professionally satisfying as such sea duty was,
you and your family are more than ready for a change of pace. The
attractions of attending a postgraduate course of instruction will be
great. The halls of academe beckon you. You may be aware subconsciously that there is hard work ahead along this path, but you are not
easily frightened and look forward to being home every night even if it
is with a briefcase full of books and class notes. One reviewer of an early

draft of this book noted, "The Navy expects that you will get your post-graduate degree on your first shore tour. If you don't you are behind the power curve."

Others recognize that postgraduate education is not for them, at least not yet. They would rather be instructors teaching in the profession of going to sea. They want to exploit their current fleet knowledge and pass it along to others. They will head for the Naval Academy, Naval Reserve Officers Training Corps (NROTC) units around the country, "Strike U" in Fallon, Nevada, the Naval Air Training Command, replacement air group squadrons at major naval air stations, or the various submarine, surface warfare, and nuclear power schools. Aviators will want to keep their hands in the flying business, building up hours and experience, and staying close to the heart of their profession. There are few preferred paths through this maze of choices.

Our objective in this chapter is to lay out some of the choices and the pros and cons to help you as you make up your mind. Of course, you will not be surprised to find that you may not have a choice; the needs of the service (you've heard that before) require that you do something not at the top of your wish list. But if you have been paying attention to your duty preference card and keeping it up to date, you have an excellent chance of getting what you want—provided you are qualified. Don't expect to get a postgraduate course in mechanical engineering if your undergraduate student record was spotty or if you were near the bottom of your class in math and science subjects.

Then we examine the many factors involved in applying for or being ordered to an instructor job and identify some of the paths that will keep you from being merely a cog in a large production machine. We wrap up this chapter by going over the implications of instructor or student duty for your fitness reports during those tours and what future selections boards will be looking for.

Assignment as a Postgraduate Student

You will not find in this book a rack up of postgraduate courses currently available or their place in the pecking order for good future assignments. Check the latest instructions on the options available, do some research, and then make sure your preference card reflects your choices. It helps your chances to have your skipper mention your suitability for your preferred courses in a fitness report no later than a year before your rotation date. Don't wait until the last minute.

In my earlier book on naval officer performance (*Career Compass*) I made the point that some care is needed in opting for a tour in the postgraduate education system. At first glance, such instruction seems like a win-win situation. You are buffing up your intellectual tools and your résumé. You are preparing yourself for important billets downstream. You may be (I use the word "may" carefully) qualifying yourself for a wider range of assignments and giving yourself the option of entering a professional specialty outside the unrestricted line. All good reasons but is there a potential downside?[2]

First, you may eventually come to realize that your postgraduate degree and classroom experience are of secondary interest to the people whose job it is to fill the Navy's billets.[3] For example, you may take a three-year course in aeronautical engineering and find that you are destined never to serve in a billet requiring such a background. Alternatively you may find yourself in consecutive shore tours that do require such a background and you wonder if you are not unduly narrowing your future prospects. In the first scenario you didn't waste your time doing a postgraduate course but you never directly applied that knowledge either. In the second scenario your postgraduate education is fully exploited but you may find your career prospects confined to a single specialty for your future shore assignments. There may be career shortcomings in both scenarios.

Second, your tour as a student will likely keep you away from your

Naval postgraduate students taking exams. While the schoolhouse setting can be attractive, a postgraduate course entails long hours of hard work. Your choice of postgraduate education and its timing can be a crucial factor in a naval career. *U.S. Naval Institute Photo Archives*

warfare community for two or three years. Your associates will be professors and other students (many from other warfare specialties), not those who will be your future skippers and commodores. The point of this cautionary sermon is that you must think through the implications of your choice to serve a student tour in the Navy's schoolhouse. It may be just right for you—or it could be dead wrong.

Finally, looking deep into your own mind and psyche, are you really cut out to be a graduate student? You want the degree but are you ready for the grinding work, long hours of study, and total commitment that a really worthwhile degree entails? Don't skip lightly over these questions and your answers to them.

Let me now turn my hat around and argue the alternative perspective. If you are to pursue a postgraduate degree (I am *not* talking now about attendance at a war college course) at some point in your career, your first shore tour is the time to do it. You simply will not have time later without accepting major career risks. Moreover, later in your career you are further away from classroom study skills gained as an undergraduate and are becoming a riskier graduate student prospect.

Now I will let you in on a secret. Insofar as engineering and science graduate courses are concerned, the odds are that in the long run it does not matter what curriculum you are ordered to. The important point is that you are attracted to it and plan to work hard to get the full benefit from the course. I firmly believe the real long-term payoff from graduate education for most naval officers—particularly in the sciences and quantitative disciplines—lies in the intellectual rigor and turn of mind they impose. You should be looking for tools to make you think better not just furnish your storehouse of knowledge. Look for the skills to be learned, not what subject matter is to be carefully stored away in your cerebral warehouse.

When the bean counters on Pentagon and congressional staffs raise their hands in disgust that the services are educating officers not destined to serve in their postgraduate specialty, they completely miss the point. For the most part the Navy is not in the business of producing professors, scientists, and captains of industry for the Navy shore establishment. The Navy education system is mostly about grooming combat leaders, and its postgraduate education system is an admirable way to hone the thinking skills needed in such leaders.

Some of this same reasoning applies to the "softer" postgraduate curricula as well. Seek out the courses and professors that challenge your thinking and offer you (in exchange for hard work) a problem-solving toolbox that has application beyond the confines of the discipline at hand. Suppleness of mind is the prize to be sought and is to my mind the biggest payoff of leaving the fleet and going back to school.

By the way, my experience tells me that officers attending postgraduate courses outside of engineering and the sciences more often get follow-on assignments in their specialty. This can be good or bad. I am thinking specifically of political-military specialists (much sought after by plans shops throughout the Navy and by joint—that is, multi-service—headquarters), financial and business management specialists (in demand by comptroller shops), and intelligence and communications specialists who are always needed in their respective communities. Many officers travel these paths to major command and ultimately to flag rank.

One final cautionary note. Don't opt for a postgraduate course of instruction just, or mainly, to get a credential in the belief that it is some type of "wicket" that you must go through in getting to the promised world of better assignments and promotion. That is a careerist's move, not one a pro makes. Opt for improving your mind and judgment—and that often is best pursued by taking a rigorous postgraduate course.

At this point you may also ask what is the career-enhancing alternative to going ashore as a Navy postgraduate student? The simple answer is to serve as an instructor or staff member in one of the Navy's many schoolhouses.

Assignment as an Instructor

These billets are all over the map. They include classroom instructors and "company officers" at the Naval Academy and assignment to an NROTC unit, the Naval Air Training Command, or to schools at Newport or New London and so on. But let's face it, some billets are more professionally enhancing, or personally rewarding, or even "fur-lined," than others are. I know of officers who wanted to be an NROTC instructor mainly because the tour gave them an opportunity to get a desired postgraduate degree on their own without incurring the associated obligated service. They already had their eye on the door out to civilian life. I know of other officers who wanted to go back to the Naval Academy for similar reasons or because their classmates were on duty there, or for its closeness to the civilian job market, or for family reasons.

Some officers want to go as an instructor in a fleet replacement squadron, or the surface warfare schools, or to the submarine or nuclear power school programs because it keeps them close to their operational specialty. They know that they will serve with the "comers" in that specialty—their future skippers, air group commanders, and commodores.

What follows is personal advice from a retired officer who served both as a schoolhouse instructor *and* as a Navy postgraduate student during his first shore tour. I believe there is little professional benefit to *yourself* after the first year or so of service in most instructor billets. That is not to say that further service in that billet is not important to the Navy. You may have to stay the additional year or two simply to meet the Navy's needs. I advise avoiding billets where the subject matter is so repetitive and unchanging that you become a cog in an educational or training machine. Pick your instructor billets (if you have the choice) not just for the subject matter but for the opportunities for professional growth and for staying close to the heartbeat of your profession—being a pro and leading others.

I will not give you a pecking order of the best jobs because the ranking changes over time, all are needed, and because most jobs are what you make of them. Look for billets that offer you an "out" after a suitable apprenticeship and payback—perhaps an opportunity to move up to a more demanding billet or to a different office in the same location.

You will be attracted to the possibilities of off-duty education while serving ashore as an instructor in the schoolhouse. You are encouraged to try it but understand going in that it will most likely be at the expense of time with your family and to your own pocketbook in most cases. It is a tough road but there are many that have done it and prospered.

Here is a checklist of questions to ask yourself before applying for instructor duty.

1. Am I asking for this assignment for personal reasons (e.g., to be near family, to pick up a graduate degree on my own, to get away from the operational environment for a while, to get better schools for my children)?

2. Does the assignment keep me close to the backbone of the naval profession (e.g., close coupling with the fleet as with the Surface Warfare School or a fleet replacement squadron)?

3. Does this assignment offer a good chance at some point of leaving the production side of education and training and moving up to its staff or leadership positions?

4. Does the school command draw the best of my contemporaries and future leaders? Or is it a professional backwater, attractive mostly to those on their way out?

5. How will this assignment make me a better department head or executive officer on my next sea tour?

6. Does this assignment offer me a realistic opportunity to undertake off-duty graduate education?

7. Am I suited by temperament to be a good instructor of midshipmen, officer candidates, or junior officers? Is this one of my strong suits? For example, am I patient, a good communicator, keenly interested in the subject matter to be taught? Am I comfortable teaching a course syllabus developed by others and not readily changed?

8. Are the minutiae of instructor duty (e.g., class discipline and motivation, grading papers, curriculum committee meetings) likely to bore me out of my skull?

9. How will this tour look to future screening and promotion boards in considering my whole record? Will I be marking time or growing professionally?

10. Can I be "sprung" readily when it is time to go back to sea or is it likely that I will become a hostage to the need to find a relief?

To answer these questions will take some personal research and require a great deal of tough self-examination to understand your motives, opportunities, and the ever-present downside of seemingly easy and comfortable choices. You should be thinking of these matters—whether to go for postgraduate instruction or instructor duty—by the second year of your first sea tour. Your most important task is to know yourself—no flip judgments—and your aspirations, limitations, and where you need work. Going with the flow is simply the worst advice you will ever receive.

Implications of Your Student Fitness Reports

Having served on a good many selection boards, I can say that most of your fitness reports while serving as a student do not draw the close attention of future screening and selection boards. First of all, if you are a student it is unlikely that your reporting senior (or those who fill out fitness report drafts for him or her) really knows much about you. Unless you are truly outstanding or become a command problem, you will be given a pass on a pass-fail system. For hot runners coming ashore and accustomed to being among the best in the comparative rankings of a fleet unit this is a real letdown. I remember asking for an appointment with my schoolhouse reporting senior (a captain nearing retirement) to discuss why I was put in the "pack" at fitness report time. He patiently explained to me that *everyone* was in the pack and suggested I go back to my books, get on with my studies, and stop worrying. It was good advice.

However, I can't leave it there. You are in school for a reason and you are expected to study and to do as well as your abilities permit. If your grades are shaky, you will invite unwanted attention. So your primary job is to do as well as you can in your courses. This is a whole different ball game from leading Sailors and being a pro in your warfare specialty. You don't have a whole lot of help; you are thrown back on your own resources—not a bad thing. You will learn how smart and how much a "quick study" you really are. This is not a Navy "punch the books and take the quiz" setting. You have to dig it out and make sense of it.

Moreover, you will be working for professors with a mind-set much different from the bluff and direct line officers you are used to following. They may prize clarity of expression but sometimes they can try your soul by seeming to talk another dialect entirely. Just as you studied your fleet bosses you will have to study your professors—coming from a completely different direction. They will be unimpressed by your overseas tours, your prowess in leading Sailors, your expertise in the cockpit or on the bridge, and the likelihood that you are going on to great things. They are interested in only one thing: your mind and how good it is. This recognition will take your breath away. Welcome to the larger world and your place in it!

Some student officers do make a mark beyond decent grades. They somehow manage to do that something extra that gets them noticed favorably. An article written for a professional journal, an article not necessarily related to the postgraduate curricula at hand. An extracurricular project that helps the schoolhouse command in some meaningful way (e.g., a leadership role in a charity drive or arranging a major command social function, teaching an off-duty course to command enlisted personnel, representing the other students on a command committee). Some of these "extras" will find their way into your fitness reports, and selection boards are quick to note that you did more than fill a classroom seat. Not a big plus but it helps set the tone as the board considers what type of officer you are.

Implications for Your Instructor Fitness Reports

In my opinion grading instructors is a more difficult matter than grading students. Unfortunately, we don't always do it well. First, there are often so many instructors serving under one reporting senior that gradations of performance are difficult to discern. Second, in a highly structured curriculum, and most are, there is often little latitude for demonstrating excellence in knowledge or skill delivery. Some reporting seniors fall back on comparative student failure rates but this is a shaky standard because so many other variables come into play. In some commands it is particularly difficult to grade because of the high quality of officer that is assigned (e.g., Top Gun, often at the Naval Academy, nuclear power school).

The good news is that selection boards recognize the problem and note only the top few and the bottom few (if any). The "pack" is simply enlarged to accommodate the many good officers serving in billets where it is generally recognized that breaking out is very, very difficult. Unless you are a marginal instructor your good sea duty reports will go a long way to getting you past in-the-pack fitness reports as an instructor. But there is some wisdom to be distilled from this practice. First, do your very best in your primary job. You are used to this at sea; continue what works at sea while ashore and instructing. What is now different is the "extra" you have an opportunity to bring to the business at hand.

Every instructor is given collateral duties. Some are better than others are. By better I mean that they give you a chance to be evaluated more closely and personally by the officers in charge. Some of these will involve a lot of hard work and off-duty time, and you will find that some of your running mates are not interested in taking on a "can of worms" where the visibility and risk of failure are high. You may not have much choice in which duties you are given, but look for the opportunity and seize it when it comes. In some training and education commands, these collateral duties assume an importance that seems to overshadow the unit's primary mission. Good classroom instruction is largely a "given"; it is the extra that gains prominence.

I remember an officer assigned as a flight instructor at a training field near Pensacola. He had heard that the command was looking for an officer sufficiently proficient in Spanish to serve as liaison officer between the Naval Air Training Command and the local Pan-American Council. That council was a local civic organization hoping to attract South American port and warehousing business to Pensacola. There were no volunteers. Hoping to improve his Spanish language proficiency the flight instructor volunteered and then had to hang on for dear life as his career took off. The first big event was a conference that drew dignitaries from all over South America, the U.S. Chamber of Commerce, the State Department, and everyone in the middle south looking for business with South America. His command received numerous requests for support and representation. The flight instructor soon found himself (a junior lieutenant) as an intermediary between his admiral (who until that point did not know he existed) and a large number of local and national interests. He heaved a sigh of relief when it was all over and he could go back to teaching primary students how to fly. What he did not know at the time is that for this service he had received some glowing fitness reports from his chain of command, fitness reports that he later learned had secured for him a shortened tour in Pensacola and a set of orders to a plum postgraduate assignment that he had eagerly sought for several years.

I alluded earlier to considering instructor billets that offered some opportunity for release from the "production line" of education and training. Upward mobility, if you will. You will find that your hands-on experience as an instructor will be even more valuable in helping your schoolhouse bosses formulate, shape, or support the program in the classroom. This deck-plate experience is a useful corrective to the pedagogues and theoreticians who develop programs from afar. Look for such opportunities to move up into management. It is a long way from being a department head at sea, but you will gain an entirely different perspective of the whole and your good qualities will become more apparent when it comes time to evaluate your performance.

It is time now to leave the schoolhouse and consider your return to sea. You return better educated, better seasoned, and well rested if you are fortunate. You are a senior lieutenant or a junior lieutenant commander and you will find the fleet different from when you left it. But before we go back to sea, we need to discuss your mental transition from being a junior officer to becoming a senior officer.

5

Transition from Junior to Senior Officer

Young studs, old fuds, and lieutenant commanders.
—Anonymous

While throughout your career you will depend on the skills you acquire as a junior officer, we should note some channel markers that you will pass on your voyage to the world of more responsible jobs and higher rank. These channel markers will tell you that you are no longer a junior officer (JO) and have entered the world of your seniors, a world that will also be yours for the rest of your cruise. What is it that is different?

The Insufficiency of Good Intentions

The first answer is that good intentions are not sufficient—and never were. Results count even as an ensign. Allowances are made for your inexperience. But such allowances are a placeholder for your steady progress. A mark of your professional maturity is a refusal to fall back on such charity. While you are accountable as a junior officer, it is not the sine qua non that it is for senior officers. You will hear some junior officers say:

- "I gave it my best shot, but it wasn't enough."
- "How was I to know?"
- "It was too hard."
- "I will do better next time."

45

- "It didn't seem important, so I didn't pay it much attention."
- "There is the right way, the wrong way, and the Navy way."
- "Something always gets (or got) in the way."
- "It's good enough for government work."
- "That's above my pay grade."
- "I am not laid-back; I just do what I am told to do."
- "I don't have a dog in that fight."

There are countless other bromides, but you get the idea. The foregoing is the equivalent of a moral shrug of the shoulders and either failing to take responsibility, looking for a way out, or offering a lame explanation. They don't work when you become a senior officer. Performing as a senior officer does not necessarily mean you have scrambled eggs on your cap visor; instead it means that you have crossed the threshold to maturity in the Navy environment. You accept total responsibility for meeting the requirements of the mission or task. Some junior officers (measured by the stripes on their sleeves) become senior officers as lieutenants—or even earlier. Others never cross that threshold, though some may slip through the mesh to make the grade of commander.

The Passivity Line of Defense

There is an old saying with a modicum of truth in it that army officers are permitted to do anything that is spelled out in the regulations and that naval officers are permitted to do anything that is not prohibited by the regulations. There is a simple point in this bit of hyperbole: you cannot simply wait to be told to get things done. Sometimes you will not be told *what* is to be done, much less how to do it. As a senior officer, or as an officer seeking such status, you must act. Not acting for the sake of acting, but acting with a purpose in mind and a plan for achieving it. What are some of the bromides used by a passive officer?

- "If they had wanted you to . . . they would have issued you one."
- "Keep one person between you and the problem."
- "Never volunteer."
- "Don't cross that bridge until you come to it."
- "Don't stick your neck out."
- "The good shoemaker sticks to his last."
- "They will tell me when they want it done."
- "It's not in the OP Order (or the night orders, or NATOPS, or UCMJ, or . . .)."
- "The only deadline I am interested in is my RAD (release from active duty) or PRD (projected rotation date)."

You get the idea. I have known many junior officers who were good at what they did (e.g., flying an airplane, standing a bridge watch) but never looked beyond the envelope to see what more needed to be done. As a bridge watch stander, you simply cannot rely exclusively on the captain's night orders. As a pilot, you cannot rely exclusively on the procedures in the NATOPS manual. The captain in his night orders and the NATOPS manual maintainers simply cannot cover every situation. They and your experience are merely starting points.

Some officers do not realize they are passive and would be offended if accused of such. They see themselves as pros that know how to do their job. But they see their jobs as closely confined by established procedures, regulations, and standing orders. Although such guidelines and directives are needed, they simply are not sufficient if you are to become a senior officer in mental outlook as well as stripes on the sleeve. This in-the-envelope thinking is necessary to accumulate the basic skills of the profession but there comes a series of points—the transition from junior to senior officer is one of them—when you must bring more to the problem than knowing the orders and following them.

I have known junior officers who knew the nautical rules of the road, the thumb rules of good ship handling, and the emergency procedures set out in NATOPS or reactor operating manuals forward and backward. They may even have had their own ideas on how they might be improved, but that knowledge was put in a remote corner of their minds as they got perfect marks on written and oral exams. Many had little interest in or mental equipment for a situation not covered in the order books.

The point is that you must be aware of "the envelope" but see beyond it to the larger world and prepare yourself to cope with out-of-the-box situations when you enter a new and unfamiliar environment. This admonition is not limited to junior officers. Many senior officers smoothly pass the channel markers in transition up to a point. Then they start to fall back on what they know and depend on, rather than preparing for and adjusting to a new situation. To use nautical metaphors: they are not prepared for a misplaced or missing marker, a marker not seen in heavy seas, or meeting a ship coming down on the wrong side of the channel.

Leading Your Officer Contemporaries—And Sometimes Seniors as Well

As a junior officer you will more often be leading your enlisted personnel and dealing with other officers as contemporaries, not seniors or juniors. You may believe that you rarely will be placed in a position of authority over other officers. In leading enlisted personnel you may be fortunate in being able to rely on good chiefs or other senior petty officers. Some junior officers see these petty officers as insulation from the real problems facing their organization.

- "If I need to know it, the chief will tell me."
- "I stay out of the chief's business and he stays out of mine."
- "The other JOs are my buddies, not my bosses. Their high regard is important to me."
- "I am loyal to my enlisted personnel and to my brother and sister officers. It is my boss's job to come to the right decisions on disci-

plinary matters. My job is to stick up for my enlisted men and women. I am not paid to do my boss's job."

- "He covers for me and I cover for him."

But you may have to lead your messmates early in your career, perhaps as an ensign. You may, through extra effort, have become qualified as officer of the deck. In that capacity you may have more senior officers as junior officer of the deck or junior officer of the watch who are under instruction. You treat them with proper respect but they are temporary subordinates. You may be a boat officer and you may not be the senior officer on board. If there is a senior officer on board, you cannot slough your responsibility off on him or her—even when they will also be held accountable.

Or, you may be a division officer and because of the vagaries of manning you may have been assigned an officer to serve as junior division officer. In these situations you are facing your first experience in leading through other officers. Some never adjust to that circumstance and try to lead them as peers.

I will put it baldly: You will never become an effective department head unless you can get the department's mission accomplished through the efforts of other departmental officers. Leading officers is more difficult than leading enlisted personnel and acquiring the skill takes some practice and advance thought. You must learn to combine the art of being a good messmate *and* an effective senior. One of the first pieces of evidence that you are making an effective transition to becoming a senior officer is that you are becoming comfortable in giving orders and direction to and through other officers. Fail that test and you have put a ceiling on your career aspirations.

I have written elsewhere about the often-posed (and usually false) dilemma between integrity and loyalty.[1] The worst mistake you can make is to put loyalty to your juniors and contemporaries above loyalty to your bosses and the command. I agree, you should not have to make a choice, but we are discussing the real not the perfect world. I have seen

junior officers go to mast with an errant enlisted person and give a glowing report on the latter's performance—a report not warranted by facts
known to the junior officer. These division officers see their principal
loyalty to their crew not their boss—who has implicitly become "them"
instead of "us." I have seen junior officers remain silent while one of
their contemporaries was engaged in a disloyal act against the executive
officer or skipper. I have heard other officers caution, "We'd better not
bring that to the attention of the skipper." And so on. If you are to make
the transition to senior officer, you must know the basics of right and
wrong and of accountability, basics you should have learned as a midshipman. Integrity works upward, downward, and sideways. They are
the vital braces that keep the business on a sound footing. Pull them
away, and the structure collapses.

Results: The Touchstone of Leadership Effectiveness

Here I do not mean results gained at the cost of trampling over subordinates (they are the key input to good results), or breaking the rules, or
by conniving for advantage against principles of moral conduct. The
goal is not results at all costs. But it is results in performance, in meeting
commitments, completing the mission, often in combat, and against all
intervening difficulties. Whiners, excuse makers, and "explainers" need
not apply. Results are what the commanding officer and you are held
accountable for. In fact another name for performance is results. If you
are not temperamentally equipped to operate in such an absolute environment, you are in the wrong business. The best may sail close to the
channel markers but they seldom go aground.

Evolving from Junior to Senior

How do you know when you have made the passage from junior to
senior officer status? You don't need a checklist, but I will provide one

anyway to let you calibrate your intuition. You know when you are making a successful transition to being a senior officer (regardless of the number of stripes on your sleeve) when you:

1. See rules and regulations as tools and not a crutch.
2. See seniority or rank as an aid to leading and not substitutes for it or as ends in themselves.
3. Are comfortable delegating *and* have the confidence that you have in place systems for monitoring the efforts of subordinates.
4. Believe "buddyism" is replaced by professional collegiality.
5. Believe the *professional* respect of colleagues and subordinates is more important than being "part of the gang."
6. Can tell colleagues and subordinates "like it is" without losing their respect.
7. Believe your ship or squadron means more to you than any one individual's regard.
8. *Routinely* find yourself doing more than the minimum required.
9. Do the things you most dislike doing, and do them well.
10. Look beyond the task or duty at hand to see how all the parts fit together.

I will close with a sea—or more accurately, a Washington—story that ties much of this discussion together. I was a lieutenant commander, a junior staff officer in the office of the Chief of Naval Operations (CNO). I worked for a crusty three-star. Our job was to represent the Navy's interests in the joint arena. One day my immediate boss (a commander) and I were so beset by seemingly conflicting directions that we sought an appointment with our three-star superior. We opened the discussion by admitting we were confused (a mistake) and asking "for guidance" as to the Navy's position on a given joint matter. We were thunderstruck when our three-star bellowed at us: "NEVER, NEVER ASK ME FOR GUIDANCE! Your job as my staff officers is to draft guidance and then get my approval. If you see my job as giving you guidance, then you must believe I am working for you rather than the other way around! Now get out of here and go to work." He was right; we had fallen into a trap of passivity. I date my transition to senior officer from that bruising office call.

6

Performance as a Department Head or Staff Officer

Doth the funnels make war with the paintwork?
Do the decks to the cannon complain?
Nay, they know that some soap or a scraper
Unites them as brothers again.
So ye, being Heads of Departments,
Do your growl with a smile on your lip,
Lest ye strive and in anger be parted,
And lessen the might of your ship.
—Capt. Ronald Hopwood[1]

You have your orders in hand and are going back to sea. In some cases the schools you will attend en route to your fleet unit will tell you that you are going as a department head; a fortunate few will have filled a department head billet near the end of their first sea tour. In other cases you may have heard from your detailer, who has talked to the receiving command's placement officer at the Naval Personnel Command, that you are slotted to be the head of a specific department. In still other cases you will have taken a call from the receiving command's executive officer congratulating you and informing you of their assignment plans for you. Welcome to the department head world.

Much is expected of you. Your solid performance as a junior officer (more often than not as a division officer) has earned you a ticket to the department head business. Moreover, good performance as a department head will ultimately lead to assignment as executive officer and probably further assignment to your first command billet.

In this chapter we discuss this new world and what you can expect, some of the challenges you will face, and the rewards that may come your way. Near the end of the chapter we will discuss staff duty, mostly fleet staff duty that may be a way station on your way to a department head billet. Never forget, however, that the objective of your second sea tour is to serve as a department head at sea. Some submariners and surface warriors will get that job near the end of their first sea tour but for you aviators this important event happens during your second sea tour if at all. Fleet staff duty may be an important stepping-stone but is not where your sights should be set.

What Is Different about Being a Department Head?

As a prospective department head you are starting to leave your junior-officer years in your wake as we discussed in the preceding chapter. As a department head you are responsible for the performance of the junior officers assigned to your department and for a major segment of your unit's readiness and mission capability. You no longer have the shield of being a fresh-caught junior officer from which less is expected. Your learning curve will be steep and forgiveness for mistakes will be more difficult to come by. Your skipper and executive officer (XO) depend mightily on you.

As a department head you will find that you spend more time in the "head shed" whether it be on the bridge, the ready room, or in your boss's offices. You are part of the board of directors of the unit. Your advice will be sought—and measured—by your superiors. Even if you are so inclined, there will be less opportunity to place blame elsewhere for shortcomings in your department.

You will find that you look at junior officers differently—even though just a few years ago you were among their number. You expect more of them and will be tempted to be impatient in the face of their shortcomings. Whereas in your previous sea tour counseling was limited to Sailors, now you find yourself instructing and counseling junior officers. You will start to gain a new appreciation of your former bosses' lament that the academy—or Officer Candidate School, or flight training, or some other commissioning program—is not turning out the caliber of junior officer that they did earlier (when they—and now you—came through the pipeline?).

Whereas in your junior officer sea tours you could look up to your department head for advice and help, now you must turn to the XO for such assistance. While in most cases such assistance is willingly given, you have acquired some professional pride and are reluctant to take that step. Moreover, the XO is busy solving problems, too. You are largely on your own and you are in charge. Moreover, you will be held accountable for missteps. You will find that mistakes made in your bailiwick are now more visible, not just to your skipper but also to your commodore or air wing commander. In short, it is beginning to dawn on you that you have entered the big leagues where being a hard charger, wearing a good uniform and a respectful demeanor, demonstrating a willingness to learn, and having good intentions are no longer sufficient. You and your team must produce—and often produce in the face of great difficulties.

You are also finding out that the Navy's work gets done mainly through people not by systems, peremptory orders, or more training and education. You will be acutely aware of the shortcomings in the people who work for you and how shallow is your department's backup capability for any given unit mission element. In times of much personnel turnover in your department you will experience a feeling of isolation and even nakedness as the wolves seem to howl at your door. But the converse is also true; you will treasure those junior officers and chiefs who carry the load professionally and without complaint, who see challenges and solutions rather than problems, and who are looking to ease your burden rather than add to it. If you are a division officer reading this chapter, your professional awareness board should be flashing lights at you. This is the junior officer you should strive to be—a trusted and able assistant to your department head, not a dead weight on the already overloaded wagon he or she is pulling. You will not only obtain the satisfaction of being a good shipmate but you also will be remembered at fitness report time.

Your Approach to Your Department Head Duties

What is the answer to the problems I have described? What it has always been: knowing your stuff, imparting that knowledge to your subordinates, training them to do the job, and then holding them accountable.

The Navy works hard to see that its department heads arrive well trained for the job at hand. The chances are that you went through a long string of associated schools before you reported aboard. But now that you are aboard you must proceed along several tracks simultaneously. You must get up to speed on your people, your systems, your mission in the context of the ship or squadron's employment schedule, and the leadership and management techniques in use or needed.

Recall in chapter 2 we examined the case of your being a division officer and possibly having to work through a weak division chief. One of your options was to go to your department head for advice and assistance. Now with your department head hat on that course is much less attractive and you ask, "Why didn't my predecessor solve that problem?" Or, "Why can't the division officer deal with it, rather than bothering me with it?" Pretty dreary stuff—and here you thought it was going to be smooth sailing with a bunch of division officers and chiefs who are as good as you remember on your first sea tour. Welcome to the real Navy where there are problems to be solved and you must do the heavy lifting!

Looking back on my own career I find that my tour as department head was the crucible that turned me into a naval officer. My systems had to perform well twenty-four hours a day and any faltering in my department quickly came to the attention of my skipper and the admiral. It was the first time that I had to stand up and be counted on for the quantity and quality of the end product, a product that was important to our task group's mission. In all candor, I found the responsibilities of serving as an executive officer and later as skipper much easier to discharge thanks to the preparation and tempering experienced during my department head tour.

A word about dealing with your chief petty officers as a department head. When you put on your department head hat one of the first things you will notice is that the chiefs seem younger than on your first sea tour. You are now a contemporary of many of them; you are not a kid anymore. You will find yourself in a more collegial relationship with your department's chiefs. You are the boss and they know it, but you will find yourself often dealing with them as equals in getting the unit's mission accomplished. A wise department head treats them with respect, seeks their advice, lets them blow off steam before getting on with the job at hand, and ensures that they know they have the key role in the department. You must decide but make every effort to get them on board before marching off. You can't fast-talk a chief, even as a department head, nor should you try. In my own department head tour, I found my chiefs to be the rock on which a solid performing organization was built. It takes work and sensitivity to make this happen but the payoff in improved performance makes the investment a good one. There is another payoff to nurturing this relationship; when you become an executive officer and later a skipper, you will have gained the necessary people skills to mold your chiefs into an effective team.

One more point. Learn to build a backup capability ("redundancy") in your organization. If you or any other person in your department becomes irreplaceable, you will be in trouble some day. Your motto is that everyone has a backup (or two)—starting with you. You will find such an approach a morale builder for the ambitious and capable subordinate and a sheet anchor when the winds of combat start to blow.

Sea Staffs

Either before or after your department head tour you may be ordered to a fleet staff (e.g., destroyer squadron, air wing, submarine squadron) for duty.[2] If you do it after your department head tour, you will be a more effective staff officer. If you do it before your department head tour you probably will be a better head of department. A few officers are ordered to more senior staffs (e.g., group commander or numbered fleet staffs). As the seniority of your staff increases, the scope of your duty as staff officer usually narrows.

One of the plusses of duty on seagoing staffs is your service as a staff watch officer. This experience will stand you in good stead if your next assignment is as a department head. You will already know how the pieces fit together as seen by your skipper's boss. You will have a better understanding of where the pressure points are on a staff (any staff) to get things done to assist your unit in achieving top performance. As good as staff duty may be for your professional development and effectiveness, never forget that you must find the opportunity to serve—and serve well—as a department head afloat.

7

How to Recognize (and Be) a "Comer"

But the ship was now in the midst of the sea, tossed with waves;
for the wind was contrary. And in the fourth watch of the night
Jesus went unto them, walking on the water.
—Matthew 14:24–25

It is time to pause on our progression through the steps to command
and examine a phenomenon that has probably come to your attention,
or will during your second tour ashore. You will notice that some of your
contemporaries and seniors seem to have gained a special reputation.
The slangy expression is "water walker." The term implies an officer
whose performance is nearly perfect, or seems so. To my ear there is a
touch of disbelief and some envy when naval officers use the term to
describe a colleague. Reaching back to the early years of the twentieth
century and up to as recently as the middle part of that century "comer"
was the term usually applied to such a high performer. When used, there
was a mixture of admiration and respect as well as recognition that the
comer had not yet arrived. He was still a work in progress but the promise of future success was evident. Note that this term antedates the great
expansion in the number of women in the Navy's officer corps.

Whether comer or water walker, officers of proven performance and
great promise always excite the interest of their colleagues be they junior, senior, or contemporary. The comers' reputations precede them. You
will hear their names mentioned in wardroom or ready room bull ses-
sions. Some observers are astonished that anyone could be so good or

lucky. Others are prepared to be skeptical. Still others attribute the comer's status to his or her support by mentors—support denied to the less fortunate. To them one's rise in the profession is primarily a political game with ability having a lesser role. But to most the reputation of a comer is a matter of healthy curiosity and generosity of spirit and admiration.

What do you care about comers except that you would like to be one yourself? My answer is that their performance, assignments, and promotions provide case studies for understanding why some officers are successful and others are not. You should be interested in what it takes to be successful in your profession. It is to your benefit to see comers operate at close range to help you observe what works and what does not in the daily discharge of their duties and yours. This leads me back to the title of this chapter: How do you recognize a comer?

The first thing you recognize is that they have an ability to get things done in the face of difficulties. They are good decision makers and they know how to handle people to get the job done. They cut through the confusion to the heart of the problem at hand. Most are good listeners; they ask good questions and listen to the answers, and when they have heard enough, they make up their minds. They are not intimidated or discouraged in the face of difficulties. Most are candid. You know where they stand. They respect their seniors—and their juniors. They demand a high standard of performance from others and themselves. They rarely are whiners and complainers. The list goes on and on—but you get the idea.

Observe a group of your contemporaries in the wardroom or ready room. Some of them have earned your and your messmates' respect. When they speak, people listen to them. When they ask you a question, it is clear they respect you and want your honest answer. They are at ease with you, their seniors, and their juniors. They do not dominate a conversation; they listen and sometimes offer the key piece of information that pulls things together. Their stock in trade is that they are recognized pros—even if junior pros. Our respect for them lies mainly in their professional accomplishment, not in what some would say is their seemingly slick manner. More often than not they have a healthy sense of humor. But their humor is usually aimed at their own lapses in judgment as contrasted with those who make others the butt of a joke. The observer soon comes to the conclusion: "These are people that I am proud to call shipmates, who deserve my trust and respect, and with whom I am comfortable. Moreover, I will seek their friendship and as circumstances suggest will inform others of my regard for them." And so a service reputation is born and expanded. *But note carefully, that it all started with becoming a pro.* Being political or lucky has nothing to do with it.

Enter the Skeptic

Skeptics will say, "Yes, it starts with being a pro but at some point luck and political skills take over the process." The skeptic overlooks the fact that at each step of the way one must be a pro. It is not enough to be a pro as a division officer; you must also be a pro as a department head, as an executive officer, and as a commanding officer. If you study closely the careers of our legendary naval leaders you will see that most were neither political nor particularly lucky. In fact in some cases they were very unlucky or the victims of politics, but they managed to overcome adversity or lack of preferment.

The skeptic may grant all this but maintain that *most* officers will make good division officers, department heads, and skippers. They continue by pointing out that politics enters into the equation in climbing the next rung of the ladder—getting good assignments where one can display one's professional wares under the eyes of appreciative seniors. In my view the skeptics miss the point: It is not enough to do a good job as division officer, department head, and skipper—one must be among the best to climb the next rung. The retreating skeptic may accept this but point out that the human (political?) element enters into the equation in getting that good assignment or being screened for the next rung. The skeptic seems to be saying:

1. The detailers are often politicized and subject to pressure from mentors and sponsors to offer the best assignments to officers whose record is no better than those of their running mates (i.e., mine).
2. Senior officers meddle in the detailing process to obtain good assignments for their protégés.
3. Screening boards tilt the playing field to benefit favored protégés.
4. Such abuses are endemic in the assignment, screening, and possibly the promotion systems.

Those who have most often leveled these criticisms or others like them are likely to have experienced a career disappointment—or are anticipating one. In almost all cases the critics do not have sufficient information to make such judgments. They know their own case very well (but perhaps not as well as they think they do) but have little understanding of the performance of their competitors in the assignment, screening, and promotion processes. They did not sit on the boards or listen to their deliberations, they did not see their performance grades in comparison with those of other officers, and they did not see the choices the detailers and boards had to make. In a sense their criticism demonstrates one or two sources of their own non-selection or failure to obtain a valued assignment: they decide on an incomplete or erroneous set of "facts," and they allowed their personal biases to cloud their perspective. They will always "operate a quart low" in whatever endeavor they take where there is competition involved.

Boards and detailers do make mistakes, just as their clientele do. But having seen the process at firsthand and as a board member, I believe the mistakes are rarer than popular biases would suggest and that when they do occur they are honest ones. In my experience when seniors meddle in the assignment process, it is to obtain the services of a desired officer for their *own* command or staff, not to grease the skids to launch their protégé to another billet their record may not support. When the latter does happen, the first question the meddling senior asks is, "How does Lieutenant Commander Smith stack up with his running mates?" As often as not the inquiring senior is chastened to learn the protégé does not stack up as well as he led himself or herself to believe and the subject is dropped.

But this diversion to discuss skepticism about comers is not the principal point of the chapter. Our interest is in understanding how comers are made and prosper to see what lessons there are for our own careers.

The Comer Phenomenon

Some comers are identified early in their careers (hark back to the wardroom scenario described above) but as often as not they come to the fore in mid career. Some are even late bloomers; they finally found a billet that allowed them to showcase their superb talents in an important mission or setting. Looking back to my own midshipman days, I can see that most of the midshipman leaders ("stripers") in the brigade, those with high academic achievement, and those with athletic prowess went on to good solid careers. What little correlation there was between midshipman achievement and the attainment of flag rank seemed to lie more in academic achievement than in midshipman rank or athletic prowess. There is no substitute for brains; but it is also clear that being bright is not a sufficient condition for success. Moreover, to confound the assessment a few made it to high rank because their other endowments outweighed any lack of cerebral sparkle.

Most often in my experience comers are identified in the middle years of a career—as a lieutenant commander and as a commander. They become well known to their contemporaries—perhaps by their early selection for promotion, but more often by the spread of their reputation in doing tough jobs well. Seniors start to seek them out for assignment to their commands or staffs. Or even more startling, they may ask the comer's advice in some cases. The comers are seen as good operators who know what is really happening on the mess decks and deck plates, what is going on at the pointed end of combat missions, and who the real leaders are (not always the admirals in charge).

Observe junior comers in social settings. More often than not savvy seniors will seek them out and pump them about recent operations or events. You may even note a certain amount of respect and deference on the part of the senior to the views of an able junior. This is not as backward as it seems. Good leaders go directly to the source of the best information and do not let disparities in rank become a barrier to staying informed. Note also that the comer in this setting is candid but respectful.

Some comers have enjoyed the good luck of an opportunity to display combat prowess early in their careers and become known; their further progress is closely watched by their fellow officers. But the staying power of such fame depends on what the officers do subsequently. Comers may get early name recognition but the rest is up to them. They can falter ("a good operational officer but we need to see what he or she does when in command"), or they can go on to a more lasting demonstration of their professional competence.

Other officers have achieved comer status by making their professional presence known early by skillful writing for professional journals or by other demonstrations of professional competence before a wide audience. I have personally observed a medium-senior officer develop and deliver a powerful briefing to higher-ranking officers; I also saw the effects of that briefing reverberate strongly throughout the chain of command—even the Navy as a whole. The briefer became something of a celebrity and repeat performances of the briefing were in high demand. The briefer became a marked person. Such prominence could be short-lived if the underlying professional credentials do not create confidence. But if the briefer had such a record, he had a splendid platform from which to demonstrate his skills and promise. Other such officers early in their careers became similarly well known to senior officers throughout the Navy and were almost by definition comers.

What It Means to You

All well and good you may say—but what does all this mean to me? Two possibilities come to mind: (1) you may have the good fortune to serve with a comer, or (2) you may in that and more remote settings draw your own lessons from a comer's performance and apply them to your own career.

In *Career Compass* I listed some points of advice to midshipmen where I stressed serving *under* the best officers you can find. You may not have a great deal to say in the matter, but if you do, exploit it to the fullest. The same advice applies to serving *with* the best officers regardless of seniority. The way they conduct themselves can serve as a daily clinic on how to become a better officer. What techniques of leadership, management, and example do they use? Could you perform as well as they do in a similar setting? What would be their critique of your performance?

If you aren't serving with comers, you can still benefit from the example they set. Unfortunately, some officers believe the secret of success is to obtain assignment to the glory road billets—as well known comers seem to have. These striving officers make a fundamental mistake in confusing assignment to a succession of such important billets with the solid performance that got the best officers to such billets in the first place. It is but a short step from angling—and failing—to get the good jobs to blaming one's lack of career success on that perceived assignment failure rather than any lack of sparkle in their own performance résumé. That is not to say you cannot benefit from knowing what are the most desirable billets and the pathway to them. But that knowledge is of limited use if the fundamental problem is your deficiency in *comparative* performance.

An Old Salt's Advice

Some of the best skippers I served under were not comers. In fact, only one of my skippers made flag. Two did not make captain and one made captain on his second go-around. They were good skippers but were not considered by their boards to be *best* suited to promotion to the *next* rank. The point is don't be unduly concerned if you serve under officers seemingly not destined for high rank. If you are fortunate to serve with or under a comer, count it as a plus and a great learning opportunity.

And here are a couple of secrets. The first one is: You stand a better chance of working for a comer on shore duty in Washington than you do in the cockpit or on the deck plates. Why is that? Not because your skipper is not first-rate, but because if you are a jewel buried on a staff in Washington you are more likely to get face time with senior officers in the many echelons above you than you are with comparable echelons in the fleet. It happens like this: As a lieutenant commander or commander way down the hierarchy in Washington, you become an expert in some aspect of your office. Your boss knows less about it than you do and his boss knows even less. Consequently, when "the man" (or woman) at the top wants to see the "expert" you are wheeled front and center and sped on your way with their best wishes. You can blow it or score a knockout—but at least you got a time at bat with the head shed. There was never a better argument for "knowing your stuff" than this. Some have made their debuts as comers in this way.

The second "secret" is related to the first. More comers seem to be identified on the basis of their superb performance in Washington than in the fleet. While it is vital to shine in your fleet jobs, such performance is expected. Moreover, you are competing in the fleet with numerous contemporaries, many of whom will also become comers. In Washington the scene changes and you are fresh from the fleet (in many instances much fresher than your bosses) and you know how things really work. You become expert in a small but very important niche in the naval profession. You may find you are not only the most junior officer in your shop but also the one with the most recent fleet experience. Solid fleet performance gives you a ticket to the game, and solid Washington performance can cement your next rung on the ladder. Poor fleet performance is rarely overcome by superior performance ashore; both are needed to secure that sought-after assignment. This applies not only to the lieutenant commander going back to sea but also to the returning flag officer.

Let us turn now to that officer who has a very important role in your career, your assignment officer, or more popularly termed "detailer." You have already come to know who he or she is. You communicate with your detailer by phone or e-mail, but now is the time to take a closer look and perhaps change some misperceptions.

8

You and Your Detailer

> Whether you found eternal bliss,
> Or sank forever to burn,
> It was nothing to do with the Pope, my boy,
> But wholly your own concern.
> —Hilaire Belloc[1]

I have written elsewhere about the role of your detailer in your professional life.[2] In this chapter we take a closer look at detailers and their workplace. Here we are not as interested in the mechanics of detailing as in the environment in which it occurs. The specifics of detailer or assignment organizations change over time. But the basic fact is that detailers are organized by warfare community within the Naval Personnel Command. Never forget the detailer represents you *and* your community. He or she directly or indirectly reports to a specific warfare community manager. That officer is a captain who is very close to the heartbeat of his or her warfare specialty. The community manager works for the Commander, Naval Personnel Command, for day-to-day assignment matters but is very well connected to the senior flag officers of his or her warfare community who are serving throughout the Navy. Needless to say the warfare community manager is an officer on the rise, knows the assignment system, and knows the community—intimately. In most cases managers have already had a very successful tour in a major command. Don't be surprised to see your community manager on the flag list in the next year or two.

Your detailer does occupy a very important role in shaping your future. But it is a mistake to believe that he or she has the decisive vote in defining the contours of that future. They are easy scapegoats when you receive a set of orders that disappoints you. Look at your assignment officer as a broker operating in the market place. Their commodity is you. If your fitness reports and assignment record sparkle, you are a very marketable commodity and many will strive to obtain your services. The detailer's job then is to broker among competing demands. They get a lot of help in all this—from you and their bosses. Never forget that it is in the detailer's and your community's interest to get you into as good a job as your performance record supports. Not only is demand on your side but also your warfare community benefits when its best officers are assigned to the best (most demanding and career enhancing) billets. Simply put, in these circumstances your detailer cannot afford to put you into a lesser job. Doing so does not serve the community, and it does not please his or her boss the community manager, or you. No warfare community wants unhappy superstars. The challenges facing that community are such that it must put its best people in the best jobs.

Why Don't I Get the Best Jobs?

The problem comes when your record, while good, doesn't have that sparkle that screams out at the reader, "Here is a comer!" Let us say that you are in "the pack" but often break out to the top side in your fitness report rankings.[3] You are a valuable commodity but you will find it somewhat harder to get the very best jobs. You may "screen" for XO or commanding officer (CO) but you may find that it is a year later than you would have liked or to a command you consider to be less than the best. Or your ranking in the screen (your detailer knows what it is) is not as high as those of your hot running contemporaries. You are still a work in progress as far as your warfare community and its associated detailers are concerned. If this describes you, your fitness reports while in command (assuming you get one) are absolutely crucial to your chances of getting the best jobs in future assignments.

The officer I have described in the preceding paragraph represents the sturdy core and strength of the Navy's officer corps. Few will get a major command or make admiral (though a wise and aggressive person never rules him- or herself out of the race), but they are the officers who make the entire organization run. If you are in this group you may encounter some disappointments in the assignment and screening business. You may find yourself in the occasional confrontation with your detailer and that person's boss as you press the assignment envelope—and in effect say: "Why not me?" It is but a short step from such frustration to blaming "the system" or the detailer or your competitors who you believe have powerful mentors. All the mentors in the world won't help you if your performance record is not better than those of most of your contemporaries. In short, there is a temptation to look to others for the source of your problem rather than looking at your own record.

Your detailer has a pretty good feel as to how you stack up in the competition—whether you are a comer, a good solid officer, a packer, or an assignment problem. Detailers will also have a pretty good idea of your chances of screening for the next assignment hurdle. In most cases detailers serve as recorders for your warfare community's screening boards.

There is a third group in addition to the two just discussed. This group is composed of officers who are in the pack but who often break out below the pack. There is a lot of talent in this group and they are essential for filling thousands of billets that make the Navy run. Their performance résumés are usually without sparkle and many do not have that extra qualification that might push them into the promised land. Often their fitness reports, when read without reference to peer rankings, suggest excellent, even outstanding, performance. However, they will not screen for the best jobs and at some point will fail to be selected for promotion in the middle grades. When these officers are measured against any absolute standard, they are very good indeed, but they are the ones who fall victim to the numbers game at screening and promotion time. Only the best are chosen, and those who are not among the best are always at risk when it comes to screening and promotion.

Assignment Problems

Many officers in the group just mentioned plan on a short career or leave early for civilian life. Most are good—but not the best as measured against their running mates. There is a fourth group but we will not spend much time on them except to present cautionary tales. This group is composed of assignment problems. Sometimes the source of these problems resides not with the officer but with his or her circumstances. The officer may not be able to accept a set of career-enhancing orders because of family health problems or other obligations. Or the officer may have to be extended in a specific locality to tend to those matters. These can be heartbreaking situations, not just for the family hardship and sacrifice involved, but also for the sometimes disastrous effects on an otherwise promising career.

A footnote: In my experience over a full career, much of it in the personnel business, the Navy I know goes to great lengths to see that humanitarian needs are met. Those who say the Navy has no heart simply have not experienced or seen the actions "the system" will take to help those in need and to do "the right thing." But at the end of the day, that same Navy has a job to do—and that job requires that qualified and available people be assigned to do it.

A small subset of the fourth group comprises officers who have a problem in their personal makeup that keeps them from being full contributors to the Navy's business. It may be (possibly undetected) alcohol or substance abuse. It may be a shortcoming from a wide variety of antisocial behaviors. It may be simply laziness or lack of effort. In other cases it may be a lack of ability or aptitude to do what is required of a naval officer. The officer acquisition and training pipeline was simply not up to uncovering their deficiencies or propensities before commissioning. I knew one officer in this group who was deservedly passed over for lieutenant commander and petitioned his commanding officer for a barely satisfactory subsequent fitness report so that he would be passed over a second time and be eligible for a cash severance payment. I knew another officer who was a poor aviator. He just managed to get through flight training and then scarcely managed to get through the fleet replacement squadron training syllabus before he was dumped in my squadron. He was a menace to everyone in the air with him and belatedly received a pilot disposition board that he should have received three years earlier. You will encounter some officers who have been carried along by the system, officers who perform only to the minimum standard. In the past they were "carried" because it was administratively so difficult to fire them. Fortunately, this problem, while not nonexistent in today's Navy, is rarely encountered.

Detailing Casualties

You will sometimes hear a naval acquaintance say, "Old Charlie was a detailing casualty." Such casualties have and probably still do occur. In its best sense it means that an officer was assigned to a billet that had to be filled and that he or she was available and so ordered. Usually the billet is important but not career enhancing. The interests of the officer seemingly were sacrificed to the "needs of the service." In the worst sense it means that "Old Charlie" sought and got a set of orders that he wanted and his detailer went along because he had a billet to be filled and Charlie was willing. The fact that the billet was not in the career mainstream bothered Charlie not at all and his detailer little more.

Almost by definition a member of the high performing group discussed earlier is rarely a detailing casualty. Occasionally, a mis-detail affects an officer in the second group (pack to above), but more often it happens to members of the third group (pack to below). But this offi-cer's performance, while satisfactory and even perhaps good by any absolute standard, was already in the running for the less-than-career-enhancing jobs, important jobs that had to be filled but were not in the career mainstream. So-called detailing casualties still occur but I would caution the reader to bring a healthy dose of skepticism in evaluating such pronouncements. Obviously the assignment system is not perfect, but it is also true that much gets laid on its doorstep that is more prop-erly attributed to less than stellar performance by the officer concerned.

There are two lessons in all this. First, your performance is the key. Second, you and your detailer are partners. Don't seek that fur-lined job that is off your career trajectory. Good detailers warn you of the conse-quences, but they cannot always save you from yourself. Ask your detailer how strong you are competitively and whether or not you are in the running and whether the job on offer will hurt or help you before the next board (screening or promotion).

Warfare Community Bosses

Each warfare community has a flag officer who by seniority, experience, and assignment is considered the head policy "honcho" for that com-munity. That person and other key flag officers in the community are in frequent communication with the warfare community manager in the Naval Personnel Command. This senior group, in effect a board of directors for the community, is very powerful in setting career progres-sion policy, the star that detailers steer by. In the Navy of twenty-five or thirty years ago such warfare bosses were usually the warfare "barons" (e.g., air, surface, sub-surface) in the office of the CNO. Today with changes in the Pentagon and flag billet structures that boss is more likely to be the senior type commander in the fleet. But four-star officers in each community, though now with major responsibilities outside their parent community, have considerable clout in shaping their warfare specialty to meet what they perceive to be the fleet's needs.

The point of this discussion is that your assignment officer is at the end of a very long chain of influence and decision that shapes the world of your warfare community and hence your prospects in it. Critical "details" (usually flag or major command assignments) will usually float to the top for concurrence and sometimes for decision, but most of the action is in the Naval Personnel Command. No matter what high-level influence may be brought to bear you must still pass muster with the screening and promotion boards. They and the record you present to them are more important to your future than any far-away three- and four-star. When you screen for major command and are selected for flag rank, the scenario changes and the Navy's and your warfare community's top leadership take a more active role in your assignments. I would argue that such role is appropriate and proper in any organization, civilian or military, where mission accomplishment is critically dependent on the quality of its top leaders.

Situational Awareness and Detailing

Earlier I said that the most important assignment in your career is the one that you now hold. While you shouldn't look too far ahead to your next or back to your last assignment, you do need to have a basic understanding of what a career in your warfare community looks like and what is required to succeed.[4] In your conversations with your detailer you need to know what you should and should not do for your next assignment.

Detailers are busy people (just as you are) but you should talk to your detailer from time to time (every six to twelve months?) just to find out what is going on in your warfare community from the personnel distribution perspective (e.g., Aegis pipeline, the coming Littoral Combat Ships). What are current concerns? Shortages, emphasis in assignments, timing of screening boards? This is a good time to impress on your detailer your active hands-on interest in your career and find out what you can do to become a marketable commodity in the assignment business. Don't wait until you are in the three-month window of receiving orders to your next assignment. As important as your duty preference card is, don't let it carry the entire load in your interactions with the personnel system.

In the next two chapters we examine the specialized cases of overseas duty and joint duty. Such assignments can be critical steps in your career and they need to be factored into your planning and expectations.

9

Performance in an Overseas Tour

Join the Navy and see the world.
—Navy recruiting posters in the 1920s

An overseas tour can be the most memorable in your career, most likely for the challenge that it presents to you and your family. But it can also be the most arduous of your career involving even more family separation, limited schooling opportunities for your children, and dealing with the frustrations induced by continuing face-to-face contact with a foreign culture.

Overseas tours come in all shapes and sizes. They could be similar to sea duty at bases stateside, where you are assigned to a ship, squadron, or staff just as you might be in the States. The primary difference is that instead of being in Norfolk or San Diego you might be in Yokosuka or Sasebo, Japan. At various times in the past thirty years the Navy has seriously considered basing carrier strike groups in Greece and Australia in addition to Japan. Another turn of the wheel could bring similar overseas basing schemes to the fore during your career as it extends out the next thirty years and beyond.

Another type of overseas duty involves assignment to an overseas staff or shore activity that does not involve going to sea. It may be duty in one of the North Atlantic Treaty Organization (NATO) nations, or on any one of the defense attaché staffs worldwide wherever the United States maintains an embassy, or with a naval support activity overseas (perhaps in Italy or Spain).

As a general rule of thumb such duty will not help you get to a department head billet, an executive officer slot, or a command tour unless your overseas assignment is to an overseas-based ship or squadron. It is work that must be done and someone must do it. Most of the time such duty will be on a staff. Some of the time it might help you fill in a joint duty requirement. All the time it will mean uprooting your family or having to endure an extended "unaccompanied" tour overseas. This downside does not mean that it is a useless tour from a career standpoint. It might have the advantages of giving you an extra dimension of familiarity with an important world region, a familiarity that will help you later in your career when such expertise is badly needed. Overseas duty may involve working for a comer in making decisions and directing operations of national importance (the staffs of Commander Fifth, Sixth, or Seventh Fleets come to mind). You may be ordered as an aide to a flag officer and observe these events at close hand.

Although I have no statistical evidence, it is my impression that overseas tours are becoming more than ever a part of a well-rounded career, that the number of such billets is increasing relative to the size of the Navy as a whole, and that more attention is being paid to filling them with quality people than was the case in years past. One former detailer recommends the factoring of such an overseas tour into your career plans and doing it early rather than late.[1] Better to do it while more junior and with fewer family responsibilities than later when there will be many competing demands for your time.

What Is Different about an Overseas Tour?

You might think that your overseas tour will be defined by the billet, not by where it is. This is true only to a point. The odds are high that your job will be defined in equal measure both by the billet and its location. You will be dealing with foreign nationals. Some may work for you, and your boss will have important official contacts with others; you will live among still others and they will help determine how you eat, live, and survive in a strange environment. Even if you are assigned to a ship or squadron overseas and your duties are largely determined by the same factors that would pertain in Norfolk or San Diego, you will find that you are supported by a base staffed and perhaps even commanded by foreigners. Nothing much will get done in official matters unless the host nation is involved. You will find that the host nation will have a key role in intermediate maintenance, supply (e.g., the food you eat, the fuel your warfare platform burns), and in deciding key aspects of your command's use of the host nation base structure.

For most officers this is a whole new ball game. Not only do you have the usual challenges of the billet, but also overlaid on those challenges and added to them is a world shaped largely by a host nation and its concerns. This complexity brings an entirely new dimension to the exercise of leadership and America's role in the world. You are heavily involved with your unit or staff. Welcome to the big leagues where being a "straight stick" but able naval officer is not enough to succeed.

As if this were not enough you are faced with cultural and language differences that impose another new frame of reference. You will start to concern yourself with things called translations and interpreters, liaison officers, host country cultural or religious sensitivities, host country and status of forces agreements, and the American ambassador to the host country. Enter the State Department, and perhaps other U.S. government agencies as well. Get the idea? Do you see that another dimension to your performance style will be needed if you are to be effective in this arena?

Where Overseas?

When I was growing up in the Cold War Navy of the fifties through the eighties of the last century, the places to be were NATO Europe and East Asia. Little attention was paid then to the Persian Gulf (we kept a small

An aerial view of the naval station in Yokosuka, Japan, in the 1990s. Because a carrier strike group is still based in Yokosuka, it is the likely site of an overseas tour for many naval professionals.
U.S. Naval Institute Photo Archives

command ship and two destroyers there) or Southern Asia in general. Times change. Today, the Middle East captures most of our attention. While that concern will continue for some years, my judgment is that the Far East and southern Asia will gradually become as important in the national security calculus. Barring some resurgence of the Soviet Union in another form, I believe Europe will continue to recede as the focus of U.S. security policy.

My advice to today's officers is to seek your overseas duty in the Far East. With a carrier strike group, an amphibious ready group, and numerous staffs based there you may have the opportunity to put in place a crucial stepping-stone to a later command tour while at the same time serving in an area that is, if my forecast is correct, likely to become even more important to our nation and our Navy in the years ahead.

While NATO still has an important role to play in regional, and increasingly in world, security (note the NATO presence in Kosovo and Afghanistan), and there are important billets to be filled on the multitudinous NATO-related staffs, these billets are generally considered to be largely fur-lined, involving service in a country not unlike much of what we encounter at our stateside duty stations. Go to Brussels, London, Naples, or Stuttgart if you must or your spouse insists—but not because that is where you are most likely to be most professionally challenged in the years ahead. Those of your contemporaries who have served ashore or have been based in the Middle and Far East are far more likely in my view to have a leg up when things heat up in those areas in future years.

The Tools You Need

Here I am not talking about the specific tools needed for the naval job content of your billet. Instead, I am addressing the mind-set and skills you need to succeed in the overseas environment. The obvious one that comes to mind is some facility with the host country language. While future members of defense attaché staffs receive government-sponsored instruction in the host-country language, most other officers ordered overseas must do this on their own. Without professional language instruction you can progress only so far, but anything you learn will be a plus. Find out from officers already in the area what works and what does not. There will probably be some off-duty language instruction where you are assigned; exploit it if you can. Most of the time you will be thrown back on your own resources. Get a phrase book and memorize the key parts of it. Read up on the culture of the place because it will help you learn the language and the customs.

In most countries any effort you make to learn the customs and language will be appreciated by your foreign hosts, colleagues, and neighbors. You will find your path less arduous than it would be otherwise. Even a vocabulary limited to asking directions and understanding the answers or one limited to ordering from a menu will stand you in good stead and increase your self-confidence in dealing with your hosts.

Some officers are able to work in an overseas ghetto or cocoon and be little affected personally by what is going on outside the compound or beyond the daily help that comes in to do household chores. In some cases you will be isolated for security reasons (some overseas jobs are in dangerous neighborhoods) but even there most of the security staff will be host-country nationals, and you owe it to yourself and your family to know what they are saying and what their concerns are.

Early in my career I spent more than two years on an overseas staff. My family and I look back on it as one of the high points of my naval service. My wife learned the language (from scratch) sufficiently well as to be able to converse with the wives (who knew no English) of my foreign colleagues and was of some assistance to my admiral and his wife in official entertaining. I had less opportunity to learn the language but every hour I spent in that effort paid off in better communications with the naval officers of the host country. What it takes to be successful in an overseas tour is a sense of adventure, an inquiring spirit, and a flexibility of mind that will, it just so happens, serve you well in any of your naval duties.

Hardships and Opportunities

There will be hardships associated with overseas duty. If you are accompanied by your family, your children will likely attend schools operated by the Department of Defense (DOD). Some of the educational opportunities you take for granted in the States will not be available. You will have few educational choices except at prohibitive expense or of exercising the option of sending your children to the local schools—or even boarding them back in the States. Some families in some localities have used local schools successfully but in this age of early preparation for ultimate entry into a good university, it is an approach with some risk.

Then, there are the hardships of finding a satisfactory place for your family to live, getting the necessary licenses and permits (e.g., operating and owning an automobile), putting safe and appetizing food on the table, dealing with neighbors with a completely different set of priorities and interests, and finding familiar forms of recreation (e.g., golf courses, camping and hiking facilities, good restaurants).

Most Navy couples stationed overseas find that opportunities lie behind most hardships. There are opportunities to travel, shop, sightsee, expand your cultural horizons that most of your civilian counterparts will never experience. If you and your spouse have narrower or different interests than those afforded by an overseas tour, you will be happy when it ends and you are ordered home.

An Overseas Tour in the Context of Your Career

Our Navy exists to defend our nation and advance its interests. Unavoidably that mission involves dealing with foreign states as friends, enemies, or as part of the backdrop of international relations. As you become more senior you will see how important foreign states are to our survival and prosperity. You will realize that there is another world out there beyond your ship or squadron, beyond your Navy, beyond the DOD, and beyond our government and its citizens. I have spoken often in this book and an earlier companion volume about a thing called "situational awareness."[2] That is, seeing the forest and the trees at the same time and shaping a course through them to mission accomplishment. One of the payoffs from an overseas tour is a greater awareness of the larger stage on which national security, the U.S. Navy, and you are players.

The DOD is so convinced of the need for such regional situational awareness that each year the current crop of new flag and general officers is required to attend the "capstone course." This course consists of six or seven weeks of travel, briefings on the world situation the United States faces, and the role of DOD components in it. The highlight of the course, according to those who have attended it, is the regional tour of overseas capitals, bases, and headquarters. In one recent year the new flag and general officers were split into three groups with one visiting the Middle East and South Asia, another going to both eastern and western Europe, and the final one traveling to the Far East. While there may be a "capstone course" in your future, an overseas tour earlier in your career goes a long way toward being a junior capstone, with the added advantage that your knowledge of your region will be in more depth and duration.

10

Joint and Combined Duty

Joint: Involving elements of more than one of the armed services.

Combined: Operations conducted by forces of two or more allied nations or services.

—Capt. John V. Noel and Capt. Edward L. Beach[1]

The Goldwater-Nichols Defense Reorganization Act of 1986 probably changed forever the way the armed services view the organization and operation of forces composed of units from more than one service. Moreover, the Joint Chiefs of Staff (JCS) were restructured to give its chairman and the combatant commands (formerly unified commands) more authority over the supervision and conduct of military operations. But there was more.

Congress, concerned about the way each service went largely its own way in training, doctrine, and integration of combat operations, directed that any officer considered for promotion to flag and general officer rank must have completed a course in professional military education (e.g., war college) and have served a meaningful tour in a joint or combined billet. While there have been some pragmatic adjustments to and tweaking of this requirement with the passage of time, Congress's intent is clear and has been taken to heart by the services.

However these changes did not occur without some grumbling and breaking of crockery in the services' cherished traditional career patterns and where and when they assign their best officers. Before the Goldwater-Nichols era there was a saying that the Army assigned its officers to the Joint Staff (of the JCS) to promote them, the Air Force assigned them there to give them a medal, and the Navy assigned them there to retire them. Not any more. A joint ticket is the only doorway to flag rank—after you have filled all the many other professional requirements of a successful career. If you don't have such an assignment before facing a flag selection board, the Navy Department has "signed in blood" a promise to send any selected flag officer to a joint billet in his or her first flag tour. Not always the best way to enter the promised land.

You may not yet be concerned about what it takes to make flag rank, but chances are that if you stay in service long enough, you will be interested at some point. I would even argue that service in a joint billet will make you a better officer in the ranks of commander and captain. What does all this mean to you? What are some examples of joint or combined billets? When should you be looking to fill that career block? What edge does serving in such a billet give you? In this chapter we respond to these questions. But first we need to clear some of the underbrush away.

First, if you are a midshipman or a junior officer this is not something that deserves your concern at this time. Your focus is still on learning your profession in your own service. Keeping your eye on the ball means never losing sight of the fact that your focus is on the stepping-stones to command and to perform superbly in each job on the way up.

About the time you are selected for lieutenant commander, perhaps after your department head tour, you may give combined or joint duty more attention. At that time your perspective is expanding and you have become more aware that there are other services out there performing missions in their own spheres that are every bit as important (well, almost!) as those assigned your service. Perhaps as an aviator you have taken fuel from a U.S. Air Force tanker or been given a vector by an Air Force surveillance and control aircraft. As a submariner you have been conscious of such things as NATO sub safe procedures. As a surface warfare officer you have become familiar, and perhaps use daily, allied tactical publications. If you are serving in an amphibious force ship, you may have lifted Army troops in an exercise. Or if you are any of the above, you may have traveled in a Military Airlift Command aircraft assigned to the Air Force. The sinews connecting the Navy to the other services are widespread and often not visible to the naked eye—or they are simply taken for granted.

By the time you are a commander and on your way to your first command, you will become very aware of joint and combined duty. With luck your joint tour is already behind you, but if it isn't, you will find that you are very pressed for time and opportunity to do everything that is expected of you on the way up the ladder. By the time you are a captain, if you have not had a joint tour, you should be looking for ways to get it if you think you have a shot at flag rank someday.

To sum up, joint or combined duty is out there in your future somewhere. If you can get the tour early without having it get in the way of your plotted course to command at sea, by all means do it. But in the short term it is not anything a junior officer should be concerned about.

Where and What Are Joint Billets?

Joint billets are all around you. Typically they involve duty on joint staffs in Norfolk, Washington, Omaha, Hawaii, or Colorado Springs. They may also involve duty while attached to another service (e.g., an exchange instructor at West Point or Colorado Springs, or an exchange pilot with an Air Force squadron). Alternatively they may involve duty at a small joint field activity. Then there is an entire overseas complex of staffs including in Europe and in the major states in Asia. Or consider the defense attaché system with offices in nearly every capital in the world. There will be no lack of billets when your time comes. A tip: If you enjoy languages and have some current fluency, you may find that you have a leg up in getting a preferred assignment to an overseas joint staff in an area of interest to you.

Combined operations are an integral part of the operating environment of the naval professional. Here the combined honor guard of USS *Theodore Roosevelt*, steaming in company with a Spanish frigate, provides arrival honors to a visiting senior Spanish officer.
Courtesy of USS Theodore Roosevelt

Combined Billets

Combined billets involve assignments to organizations that comprise members from more than one state. For example: NATO staffs in the United States and overseas, or Korea, Europe, or in the Middle East as this is written. These jobs require a blend of a joint mind-set together with an overseas mind-set described in the previous chapter. Which are better, combined or joint jobs? Often combined staff jobs will involve joint matters as well. I don't know of a single set of best jobs. My bias is toward assignment to the Joint Staff of the JCS in Washington. A caveat: There are good joint or combined jobs and there are something less than good ones. The best involve current operations or major planning responsibilities. The worst involve a narrow field of expertise or are far removed from the action. Combined staffs in particular often involve a laid-back approach to planning and contingency responsibilities that involve more negotiating than military planning.

In earlier years some NATO staffs were backwaters where little got done, there was little sense of urgency, and the primary rationale for the staff was to ensure each nation got its share of the NATO command structure. I have seen some such staffs at close range and the sight was not reassuring. Working hours were a laugher by Washington standards. Moreover, some states assigned officers to those staffs to enjoy the perks of duty-free merchandise, special allowances, and so on. You get the picture. In many such staffs the British and American members did most of the heavy lifting, but my assessment was and is that most of it was wheel-spinning. If this sounds attractive to you as a professional option, you may put down this book right now for you will get little more out of it.

The Flag Connection

Completely aside from the law that requires that each officer selected for flag must have served in a joint or combined billet on the way up, there is another facet of this practice. An inordinate number of flag billets involve joint or combined matters even if not part of a joint or combined staff. The required prior tour is invaluable in making you more effective while serving in such billets. Flag officers find that friendship with officers in our sister services pays off not only in a better understanding of those services but also in nurturing a valuable set of contacts to get things done across service lines. Officers with such a "purple-suited" reputation are much sought after when it comes to important flag details, including for very high rank.

In my own career I served in units under the command of Italian and Royal Navy flag officers. I found that the experience was invaluable in understanding the opportunities and difficulties of combined command. Along the way I formed friendships that served me well later in my career. You may have the same opportunity and profit from it.

11

Serving as Executive Officer

Number one: The Royal Navy term for executive officer

Serving as executive officer is one of those anomalies of service life where even though you aren't in charge or command, you nonetheless have major responsibilities and often act for the commander.[1] You are part of the "head shed" but are not yet the boss. You are permitted no close friends in the command yet loyalty is the key virtue—in this case loyalty to your commanding officer. Your job is converting the skipper's commands and policies into actionable orders and procedures and seeing that they are carried out. The unit's department heads work for you—but they are granted direct access to the skipper. Your job is to unburden the commanding officer so the skipper can fight the ship or unit without the necessity of actually performing most of the day-to-day details of running the ship. In short, the executive officer is the officer in the middle—the bridge between the skipper and the wardroom and the mess decks. Bridges, if they are to serve their purpose, sometimes get stepped on.

Welcome to a tough job, a real test of your leadership ability. You are the officer in charge of difficulties who must fashion a serviceable link between what is and what must be. You will find that you spend a great deal of time with the captain, getting direction and providing feedback. You will show up on the bridge with a sheaf of papers to discuss with the captain. You will hold executive officer's screening for captain's mast (nonjudicial punishment). While you may not impose punishment, you must ascertain the facts—and in many cases institute corrective action that falls short of punishment. It is you who decides when the ship's work is done and officers and crew may go ashore. You will find able department heads testing you for advantage (for their departments, only rarely for themselves) and sometimes infringing on your prerogatives. Moreover, some skippers may also encroach on what is normally your turf. At the end of the day you are likely to do the most in setting and enforcing standards of smartness for your unit. Visitors to your ship or squadron can look around its spaces and see quickly your degree of diligence. I have observed visiting flag officers seeking out the host executive officer of a crack ship to congratulate that officer on the obvious high standards of cleanliness and smartness. The news of your ability will rapidly spread along the "waterfront"—that key location for your professional reputation.

Most commanding officers will stay out of *how* you do your job but they will be watching you closely nonetheless. You have the only job in the ship or squadron where your and the skipper's *scope* of responsibility are identical. You aren't the skipper but you act for him or her in most cases. You will find yourself dragged down by paperwork and administration, yet somehow you must find the time to keep your ship handling and tactical skills honed. Skippers expect you to be able to relieve them on the bridge or represent them to their bosses when they are not in a position to do so. This load of demands on the executive officer's time and stamina are a test of that officer's qualifications for future command. It is very rare in today's Navy to be ordered to command in the grade of commander without having served a previous tour as executive officer.

Differences in Assignment Practices among the Warfare Communities

Naval aviation short-circuits the path to command as applied by the other warfare communities by fleeting up executive officers and deputy air wing commanders to relieve their bosses when the latter are reassigned. This practice results in economies (eliminating a great deal of retraining time) and puts in place in the command a fully qualified potential relief for the current skipper.[2] In contrast to the aviation practice where both the squadron skipper and the executive officer are in the rank of commander, submarine and surface warfare executive officers are one (sometimes two) ranks junior to their skippers. Moreover, unlike the aviation practice submarine and surface warfare officers attend a prospective executive officer course at their respective warfare schools before assuming their duties aboard.

The reasons for the difference in assignment practices lie largely in the different histories and traditions of the three major warfare communities. In aviation squadrons almost every officer has a flight duty—whether skipper or boot ensign. And flight leadership duties are often alternated with little regard to rank. A skipper's performance grades for landing on the carrier and in weapons delivery are common knowledge and readily compared to those achieved by the most junior officer in the squadron. The aviation skipper is not a remote figure on the bridge or in his or her sea cabin but often a flight leader or temporarily a wingman who receives most of the same training and indoctrination as his or her most junior subordinate. This relationship leads to a greater degree of informality with regard to rank distinctions (though there is no doubt as to who is in charge). One result has been that the aviation community has had no difficulty with the fleet-up concept of an executive officer (who meets the standard) taking over as the next commanding officer of the same squadron.

In my experience skippers and XOs in fleet squadrons tend to have relationships like those between siblings. I have never met an aviator serving in either one of these billets who was uncomfortable with this arrangement. One bit of fallout is that the level of experience at the top in aviation squadrons is higher than it is in the shipboard communities.

In the shipboard communities there has traditionally been greater distance and more formality between the skipper and his or her executive officer—even in small ships. While the XO attempts to qualify for command and might in a pinch have to relieve his or her boss, the XO's own command opportunity lies in the future in another unit. This is also the case with the command of aircraft carriers—where the XO may also be an officer serving in the rank of captain but must complete successfully a deep draft command tour before being qualified for a carrier command.

Ship captains have always been more remote and treated with more formality than skippers of aviation squadrons. As one definitive source puts it, "The successful commanding officer, then, must learn to become as one with his or her wardroom; yet, at the same time, he or she must remain above and apart."[3] This "apartness" means that a fleet-up of a surface or submarine warfare XO to CO is a great rarity and usually a stopgap until a new skipper can be ordered in. Aviation squadron XOs are already screened for CO, while in surface and submarine warfare units they rarely are.

You might ask what is the significance of these community distinctions for the performance of their subordinates (i.e., you as the XO). Aside from gaining an understanding of the pros and cons of these assignment practices, your own path to your next assignment and promotion should be clearer. For junior surface and submarine warriors your next step after a good tour as a department head is to screen for XO. For aviators, the next step is command screening wherein you know in advance you will serve a prior and immediately adjacent tour as an XO of the same squadron.

What Skippers Want in an Executive Officer

One successful skipper described the XO's challenge this way: "OK, Captain, your vision says this, so that means we have to do this every Monday, Wednesday, and Friday—and I have to figure out how to get everyone to like it."[4]

A ship or squadron with a superb XO runs like a smoothly oiled machine. Routine things are taken care of routinely with a minimum of fuss. The command is prepared to handle the nonroutine. The good XO keeps the skipper shielded from the minutiae of administration and personnel management but is sensitive in identifying the seemingly routine that must be brought to the skipper's attention. The ship or squadron spaces are clean and shipshape. A good balance is struck among operations, training, and maintenance. When absent the skipper feels comfortable in leaving the XO in charge. The good XO anticipates problems and solves them, avoiding the need for costly remedies and distraction. You get the idea; but you may well ask—what guidance do you have to help me achieve all these goals? Isn't there anything you can tell me to help me get off to a good start in this demanding assignment?

I will give you a few stars to steer by. First and vitally important is that you and your skipper must read off the same sheet of music—the skipper's music, not yours. There is nothing that will get you off to a rocky start faster than having your own agenda. You and your skipper should be like hand and glove. You know in detail what the captain's policy is and you are that officer's champion in the ring with the wardroom, the chiefs' mess, and the mess decks. Your skipper will take great pains to see that you understand what the policy is and will mark out the shoal water for you. Listen closely; this is not boilerplate; it is twenty-four karat guidance.

During your turnover with the officer you are to relieve, identify those areas you want to discuss with the skipper as you take up your duties. While you are expected to innovate and bring new tools and style to bear on your job, you need to bring your skipper on board before embarking on bold new initiatives. I know of new XOs who looked around their unit and decided drastic measures were needed to square things away. Go ahead, look around, and figure out what you want to do, but get the skipper's concurrence if major changes are contemplated, and then go on and charge! Remember, it is your job to help put the skipper's stamp on the command, not your own.

A second important point. Don't be the lone ranger. You will be swamped if you try to do or change things single-handedly. You must get your orders to flow through the department heads. Your principal job, other than keeping the skipper happy, is to see that the department heads are pulling smoothly on your wagon as well as their own departmental wagons. Some department heads will just want to be left alone and will consider the XO's workload as of only passing interest to them. Wrong thinking on their part. You prospective department heads reading this, take heed. You are the XO's teammates and that officer is not just another power center you have to deal with. If you aren't pulling smoothly with your XO, you aren't doing a complete job no matter how well your department shines or how many *E*s it has won.

Third, a critical aspect of the XO's job is to plan and delegate so the *entire* ship's workload gets done. If the departments are to pull together effectively they need coordinating mechanisms besides the plan of the day and the eight o'clock reports. These mechanisms include plans for schools, onboard training, conducting exercises, and preparing for key inspections, maintenance, and upkeep. A large number of "stove pipes" (e.g., self-contained workloads) and individual managers of specific tasks may be necessary but certainly are not sufficient for the well-run unit. Any XO overlooks or delegates this coordinating function at his or her professional peril.

Finally, don't forget you are preparing yourself for future command. If you concentrate solely on being a manager in charge of "heads and beds," you will let both yourself and your skipper down. You must be ready to relieve your skipper on a moment's notice—and you won't be ready if paperwork or routine "inspect and correct" items are your primary concerns.

What Subordinates Want in an Executive Officer

The first thing they are looking for is consistent and decisive guidance and orders. They will be quick to detect any gaps in the solid front expected of a skipper and the executive officer. The more opportunistic subordinates may attempt to exploit those gaps to their partisan (departmental) advantage. They expect the executive officer to be a model of loyalty and decisiveness. Yet they also expect the XO to be an interpreter of orders and policies, someone they can talk to about the details of implementation if the policies seem ambiguous or not applicable to the situation at hand. The ideal XO is approachable but not a nanny.

Some subordinates will attempt to use the XO as a buffer between themselves and the skipper—or to use a horrid phrase, "delegate upward," by trying to make the XO responsible for difficulties experienced in their own department. This situation will require a firm hand by the XO in reminding subordinates of their departmental duties and their necessary contribution to the unit's performance.

Subordinates are also looking for a fair XO who does not play favorites among the departments and keeps an open mind in the face of disagreement and requests. Favoritism may take several forms. In one case the XO may tend to favor a department because of his or her own experience in a similar department. In another case the XO who has such experience may exert undue influence within the department in which he or she has served previously. In still other cases an XO may defer unduly to departments in which that officer has little experience. All these and other biases represent shoal water.

Subordinates are also looking for an XO who is good at team building. They want to be led, and they want clarity in orders. Most also want a feeling of comradeship with their brother and sister officers. The XO must work hard to create this chemistry. He or she does this by hearing people out, keeping emotions in check, and ensuring the skipper is informed and agrees with the direction the XO and department heads are taking.

Department heads expect the XO to help them in sounding out the skipper on proposals for change in policy that they believe will work to the unit's overall advantage. Care is needed here. The executive officer is not a special pleader. However, that officer has the major role in interpreting policies and orders to put them in actionable terms, and to ensure the commanding officer is aware of concerns, proposals, ideas, and problems that bear on the unit's effectiveness. This is a two-way street but needs to be maintained with tact, firmness, and loyalty both ways. As executive officer you are not a diplomat negotiating between foreign powers, but you need to be sensitive to the mission of the command and the proper role of each player in meeting the requirements of that mission. Welcome to the world of leadership above the deck plates.

Most of the Navy's work is not done by peremptory orders (though they sometimes are needed), but by clear thinking, good will, and a keen understanding of the fact that real people with all their skills and imperfections do the work. The good executive officer is in the center of this calculus and that is the reason service in the XO job is a prerequisite to later assignment to command.

Before ending this chapter a word needs to be said about the occasional subordinate who will knowingly or unknowingly end-run his or her XO. Department heads by regulation have direct access to the skipper. But as a matter of courtesy and long service tradition they have an obligation to ensure the XO is informed of matters being taken to the skipper. I don't mean, "Oh, by the way, I plan to tell the skipper about our plans to streamline the departmental watch organization." I mean going over in some detail any proposals or reports that have spillover effects on other departments or could prompt fundamental changes in the unit's routine and practices.

The inadvertent end run is more likely than the breaches just discussed. A department head after briefing the XO on the way to see the CO will sometimes get in a subsequent discussion with the skipper that leads to broadening the issue being examined. This is dangerous water: the department head must be quick to indicate the need to discuss again the subject with the XO before seeking or getting the skipper's agreement. Most skippers have a keen nose for end runs and will work to keep discussions within proper boundaries.

Another Navy tradition is the "back brief." If a subordinate is summoned to discuss something with the skipper without a prior opportunity to discuss it with the intervening chain of command, the subordinate has the solemn obligation to ensure his or her chain of command is promptly and fully informed of the content of the discussions conducted. Most of this is common courtesy based on recognition that sometimes the skipper needs a fast response. But a junior gets a reputation for being an opportunist or slick at some peril. Even the *appearance* of such conduct must be shunned or quickly put in context for those most affected.

When you finish your stint as XO you will be able to look back on a tour of hard work and being put on your mettle. You should also feel that you are ready for command and in most cases your skipper will have recommended that you be assigned one. Nothing that is really worthwhile in this life is easy to obtain. Your good tour as XO is one of the prices you pay to get the long-sought command tour.

12

Brothers and Sisters in Arms

We few, we happy few, we band of brothers;
For he to-day that sheds his blood with me
Shall be my brother. . . .
—Shakespeare, *Henry V*

Very early in your naval career you found out that the Navy is divided not just between the Pacific and Atlantic Fleets but also among the various warfare communities such as surface, air, and submarine warfare. As if that weren't enough, there are subcommunities in each. Each community has a special outlook and ethos, is proud of their role in national security and the Navy as a whole, and in the secret recesses of its collective mind believes its brother or sister communities are not quite up to the standards set by their own community. To highlight such distinctions and esprit de corps are helpful in fostering professionalism. Esprit prospers if there is a rival at hand and the "us against them" spirit helps bond members to one another.

However, at times such splitting and "unionizing" in the naval service goes too far and we suddenly find at mid career if not earlier that we need each other and each community brings something to the fight against a common enemy. Most of your sea duty through the grade of commander will be spent in your own community. You will know its leaders and some of them will know you. Its senior members fill out your fitness reports, sit on your screening boards, and can (if your record warrants it) be your champions when promotion boards meet.

But even before you reach the rank of commander there is a good chance that you will have served with members of other communities on fleet staffs or in shore billets. You start to realize how it all comes together. This early splitting and later blending is probably inevitable and even healthy. But it is the wise officer who knows early where his career train is headed and doesn't wait for the vagaries of the assignment system to put it together for him or her.

The Warfare Subcommunity Phenomenon

A sometimes bothersome derivative of the community system is the further subdivision into included communities. In surface warfare it is cruisers and destroyers, amphibs, and "all others" (tenders, a few replenishment ships, miscellaneous auxiliaries). In aviation it is fighter-attack, antisubmarine, helicopters, early warning, and aviation logistics units. In submarines it is attack and the SSBNs ("boomers"). Add to these "trade unions" mine warfare (composed of air and surface units) plus special warfare (a community of its own) and the way its units are delivered to the battle area (submarines, air, amphibs). The principal reason for these narrow specialties is the increased complexity of modern weapons systems and the need to reduce retraining costs. However, a side effect of this "stove-piping" of the warfare communities is its spillover into promotions as some specialties enjoy better promotion rates—particularly to captain and flag rank.

Some—in a self-serving way—explain this differential by stating that the best people are assigned to the preferred warfare platforms and it is not surprising that their promotion rates are higher. Others say that it is a self-perpetuating system of preferences, that those from the preferred communities predominate on selection boards and tend to pick their own. Still others say that the explanation goes deeper than glib justifications and goes back to what the Navy's leadership views as the optimal career progression and what qualifications are needed to lead a particular grouping (e.g., carrier strike groups).

For example, during most of the Cold War it was considered unthinkable by the Navy's top aviators to have any officer other than a member of the fighter-attack community command an attack carrier or carrier air wing. Most of naval aviation's top leadership came from that community. But the specialization went further. Until the mid seventies it was considered unthinkable to have naval flight officers ("back seaters")—even though members of the fighter-attack community—command aircraft carriers. The surface warfare community has experienced similar (if different in the details) biases in differentiating between cruiser-destroyer officers and amphibious trained officers.

This phenomenon has over the years resulted in what I call orphan communities, communities that are disproportionately underrepresented in promotions, particularly to flag rank. At one time women officers were considered second-class officers in the assignment and promotion business because by law they were prohibited from going to sea or into combat. Later, naval flight officers were second-class officers (behind pilots) in screening for command and promotions. Still later helicopter pilots and carrier antisubmarine warfare officers were disproportionately underrepresented in the Navy's top aviation ranks. At the same time that these preferences existed, surface warfare officers with a career in the amphibious forces fared worse than cruiser and destroyer officers before selection boards. I can't speak for historical practices in the submarine force but I do know that during the transition to nuclear power in that force, well-qualified diesel submarine officers were considered second-class citizens in the assignment process and were somewhat roughly handled at promotion time.

Fortunately these practices either have changed or are changing. Thirty years ago it would have been unheard of for a naval flight officer or helicopter pilot to command a carrier or an air wing. Not so today. Women officers weren't even in the race (by law). It was not uncommon for amphibious groups to be commanded by aviators or destroyer officers with little if any prior experience in amphibs, there being so few homegrown amphibious-trained flag officers. Similarly when we had antisubmarine warfare task groups some of their admirals were fighter pilots with no experience in antisubmarine warfare. All this is gradually changing for the better, but for midshipmen reading these pages, let no one tell you that the warfare community you pick (or are drafted into) and the ship or aircraft type you plan to operate does not have an important impact on your future promotability. Times change but old patterns die hard. Service selection is one of the crucial milestones of your career and it comes early—before you really have your sea legs and know how the service works. We discuss this subject in more depth in appendix A.

The Other Services

This book is not the place to make or refute the arguments as to why we have separate armed services. My own biases are that the current delineation of roles and missions and service boundaries are about right, though there are fierce arguments among the services over where the boundaries meet, particularly in the command and employment of air forces. The point to be made here is that professional officers are well served by gaining an understanding of their brothers and sisters in arms from the other services. You will serve with them, you will go to war with them, and some of you may die with them. They are officers much like yourselves: proud of their service and their country, with strong bonds to their comrades, and working hard to become professionals.

You will best gain this understanding by attending a war college course, particularly the Joint Forces Staff College in Norfolk or the National Defense University in Washington, D.C. The service war colleges make a determined effort to deal with their sister services fairly but the makeup of the student body and faculty works against such "purple suiting."

A key experience in my own career was attending the five-month course at the Joint Forces Staff College (then the Armed Forces Staff College) as a lieutenant commander. I gained an appreciation of what the Army, Air Force, and Marine Corps were about, an understanding that carried me through an entire career. Even today in retirement, I have occasion to draw on that experience of some forty years ago.

Allies as Brothers and Sisters in Arms

This is a more complex relationship because it hinges on the political alignments of the era. It lies more in the politico-military realm than as an element of the professionalism of the officer corps. One set of bonds that has remained unchanged for almost a century is our collective relationship with the Royal Navy and the Commonwealth Navies—particularly those of Australia and Canada. In my lifetime those bonds have been close—based on a common heritage and a shared understanding of the meaning of control of the sea. Those bonds have been tested and tempered in the heat of battle as comrades in arms. Any U.S. naval officer will be welcome in any Royal Navy wardroom and that hospitality will be fully reciprocated in our ships.

As you become more senior you will experience the bonds of personal friendship with officers of the Royal Navy and its Commonwealth sister services. I have seen instances in my own career where these bonds made for a more effective fighting force than would otherwise be the case. I know of no more rewarding experience than in going to sea in peace or war with these comrades.

13

Navy Friendships

> There is no friendship that is as deep and lasting as that
> between shipmates, particularly those who have gone to war
> together and share a proud memory of service.
> —A retired officer

One of the glories of civilized life is the forming and nurturing of friendships. Some friendships date back to university or academy days— and a few even earlier. In a Navy setting friendships can be the result of being shipmates, classmates, neighbors, fellow members of a church or synagogue, or from one officer being a mentor to another. In the Navy friendships are most often with contemporaries but often cross lines of rank and seniority, and over time even officer and enlisted status.

A distinctive characteristic of Navy friendships is that they endure for years, decades, and entire lifetimes because of the closed nature of the service environment. Not closed in the sense that others may not enter, but closed in the sense that future assignment patterns and home ports seem to intersect and the opportunity to renew friendships results. To a degree the Navy is family. While there are several hundred thousand active duty members of that family, at times it can seem very small when you often have brief encounters with old friends and catch up with others, or you end up assigned to the same strike group or shore station.

The bonds of Navy friendships are "tight" because they often start with a set of shared experiences—some not that pleasant—perhaps service together on a deployment, perhaps as neighbors in adjacent sets of government quarters, perhaps as a result of Navy spouse-to-spouse interactions in a home port, perhaps service together in sister ships or sister squadrons, and so on. I remember as a commander being ordered to a two-week school overseas. We had two young children; a Navy friend and spouse volunteered to keep our two children if my wife could accompany me. She did, they did, and we had a marvelous experience in a once-in-a-lifetime opportunity. We have repaid that debt to others in my Navy career. This kind of thing occurs all the time in a Navy setting. If a spouse has a chance to "ship-follow" (joining the ship in one or more overseas ports), it is common to see friends close ranks and find a way to keep the children while their parents are absent.

As you follow a Navy career, you will find that you are occasionally a shipmate with danger and death. You will lose friends and shipmates either to operational accident, or enemy action, or simply driving home from work. Or a service family may be struck by a major illness. In these situations the Navy community of friends and shipmates comes together in ways that might seem incomprehensible in civilian communities where sorrow and support are largely limited to family, fellow church members, and perhaps a few close friends. Navy families have no difficulty seeing themselves in the stricken family's situation.

Academy graduates experience a special kind of friendship. That ring of friendship is extended to most of their academy classmates. Class bonds are very close and most members regard their classmates as the civilian equivalent of fraternity brothers or sorority sisters. These friendships endure for a lifetime and beyond as surviving spouses are enfolded in the community. Because the Navy is a community that promotes from within its ranks and requires that its members move to new duty stations from time to time, class bonds are continually reinforced. For non-academy graduates reading this, please don't come to the conclusion that there is a ring knocker mentality that excludes others, or that there is a "secret handshake" that seals others out to their professional detriment. No, what you are seeing is uncomplicated friendship started on the banks of the Severn for four years and then nurtured through years of service together.

In another context I have noted that submariners and SEALs seem to form a similar bond. Perhaps this is because the communities are relatively small compared to the others. Or perhaps it is because SEAL teams and submarines have small personnel complements that foster close friendships and professional relationships. Or perhaps it is because the training pipelines are so rigorous that special bonds are formed in the doing. This closeness is not a reproach or threat to members of other communities. Rather, it is pride in a close association forged under demanding circumstances.

Friends and Rivals?

I am sometimes asked, "Aren't Navy friendships inimical to good order and discipline?" How can you be a friend to a senior or junior without seeming to work to the prejudice of others? Can a friend be a rival at the same time—and how are such relationships handled? The simple answer to all these questions is that friendship doesn't get in the way of official relationships and officer performance. Rather, friendship is a separate realm that often cements relationships between professionals but does not replace or shape those relationships.

Of course, when friends are in the same unit some care is needed to ensure the personal does not spill over into the professional. You may be fellow department heads with each striving for that number one early promote fitness report—but remain friends. Time after time in my own career, I ran with a fine bunch of pros who were also my friends. I should make it clear that often they received the skipper's top fitness report. If anything, I believe such friendship enhanced rather than degraded unit performance. A skipper who has a group of department heads who are friends and stay friends (as most do) is truly blessed and will have a command that is pulling together. I have experienced instances where one friend pulled another's bacon out of the fire and saw that favor reciprocated later in the tour.

The secret of competing with friends and keeping them as friends is to look to your own performance and not focus on what others are doing. *Don't permit yourself to look over your shoulder.* Be a player not a referee. And lend a helping hand to others crossing the finish line.

Friendship with Your Sailors

You will be tempted to form friendships with Sailors in your unit. But that must wait until you are no longer serving together. You simply cannot give even the appearance of a special relationship with subordinates while you are in charge. There is no mystery or anything snobbish about this. You will find yourself in a position where you must make hard decisions about your Sailors, decisions that friendship may compromise. It is in later years that friendship can pick up where official relationships left off. The Internet and e-mail have made this process much easier.

In my own experience I served with some outstanding Sailors and in the years since our joint service our friendships have prospered. I happen to enjoy ship and squadron reunions (you probably will, too). Each year I attend at least two. Out of these reunions and recalling our times as shipmates a lively correspondence has cropped up that both parties seem to enjoy. One of these former shipmates, a boatswain's mate second class, went on to a career as an animator for Disney Studios and as a token of friendship he designed the cover of a book I authored some years ago. I look forward to repaying the favor. Another friendship involves a retired chief radarman who I qualified as an OOD in my ship—probably a first in our squadron. Still another involves a senior chief petty officer who served as my maintenance chief when I was maintenance officer of a carrier-based squadron. Still another is a radarman third class in my first ship assignment who stood in for me as combat information center watch officer while I emptied a seasick stomach in a nearby head.

Some junior officers have a keen desire to be popular with their sub-ordinates. Your chief will discourage this but you may be tempted to press on and become one of the boys or girls. *Be warned that only the very worst officers succumb to this temptation.* They have fallen for the false Hollywood portrayal of the beloved skipper or division officer. No one who has been a real Sailor will ever fall for this lure. When you go to war you want to be led by a pro, not by Mr. or Ms. Popularity. You will be a good shipmate to your Sailors and foster mutual respect, but friendship must wait.

Friendship with Your Seniors

Such friendship usually takes the form of a mentor relationship and it often starts with your skipper or other boss taking special interest in your performance and career development. But he or she will be very careful to keep official relationships official because they must be concerned with the performance of the department or unit as a whole and not play favorites. Typically such mentoring matures after you or your boss have been detached. In an earlier book on naval officer performance I wrote at length about mentoring and will not repeat it here. But I should raise a caution flag.

You will notice that most if not all skippers or bosses will address you by your first name. The reverse is, of course, not in order. There was a time in my professional lifetime when officer subordinates were addressed by their superiors only by their last name or by the term "mister" or "miss" (in those days). Like much social coinage the old usage was debased to a more informal form that seems to fit better with the mores of modern society. But don't for a minute believe that because your skipper or boss addresses you by your first name that you are his or her friend. Not yet, anyway. Seniors will have occasion to chew you out (the more modern term is "counseling") but don't think that because they use your first name on such occasions that they are counseling you as a friend. You are being "wire-brushed" as an errant subordinate.

Moreover, your skippers are not social workers who are inordinately concerned about your "feelings," perceived inadequacies, or your self-esteem. They are interested in whether or not you are pulling the wagon, doing your duty, and growing professionally. Friendship has absolutely nothing to do with it.

Friendships and Performance

After this discussion of friendships in a Navy setting you may be asking, "This is all well and good, but what has it got to do with a naval officer's performance?" The simple answer is that friendships in the profession are one of the many sinews that tie you to the institution and enhance your performance in it. The other sinews are esprit de corps, comradeship, mentorship, and family support. The Navy is more than ships, airplanes, machinery, and shore stations. It is operated, maintained, and led by human beings—all of whom are volunteers. The human dimension is what makes the whole thing work. Call it chemistry if you will. But you will be quick to notice the absence of what I here call sinews of the service. It is inconceivable to me or any Navy man or woman I know to envisage a ship or squadron—or Navy—operating well without friendships among its members. But you must know the rules: (1) duty first, then shipmates, and yourself last; (2) look to your own performance, not how others are doing; (3) extend the helping hand; and (4) inclusion, not exclusion.

14

Social Polish

It is by no means enough that an officer of the Navy should be a capable mariner. He must be that, of course, but also a great deal more. He should be as well a gentleman of liberal education, refined manners, punctilious courtesy, and the nicest sense of personal honor.
—John Paul Jones[1]

Some readers have already read my earlier sermon on the need for social polish in your sea bag.[2] If you lead others, and that is what a naval career is all about, you need to learn about and use the grease that lubricates the gears of interpersonal relations. You need to know what behaviors comprise good manners; whether you use that knowledge or not is up to you. Your observance or lack thereof will serve you either for good or ill. Let me be clear: I am not talking about the punctilio of formal etiquette such as making calls, leaving cards, social precedence, seating at formal banquets, and such like. Older service etiquette books spent a great deal of time on these subjects. Old-timers may mourn the diminished relevance of these graces but the fact is that such subjects seem to have little place in today's military setting. Rather, I am talking about getting things done easily, efficiently, and "with class" through people and the attributes that make such results possible.

The Use of Good Manners Is Not Limited to Social Occasions

Some have a set of good manners that they break out for social occasions and then put them back in the locker until they are again needed. Good manners are a 24–7 set of tools that are used as much in the work place as on the social scene. The real master of good manners can administer a tongue lashing to an errant subordinate without straying over into boorish behavior, the use of profanity, or loss of temper. The essence of good manners is to respect others even if you disagree with them or must administer an official reprimand.

In this chapter we go beyond the basics of such conduct to examine some of the finer points in a naval setting. But first, let us review some basics in your dealings with others whether they are subordinates, contemporaries, or seniors.

1. *If you have to raise your voice, you are lowering the esteem in which others hold you.* Concentrate on keeping your voice under control. Some direct orders have to be crisp, firm, and distinctly audible ("Left full rudder"). But for the most part the Navy's business can be conducted in a conversational tone of voice. Some officers when agitated not only raise their voices but also start to accelerate their delivery and slur syllables. Their intent seems to be to overbear or cow their listeners—a sure sign that communications are starting to deteriorate.

2. *Be a good listener.* One of the cardinal mistakes in communicating is to keep pressing the send button and overlook the fact that any discussion is a two-way street. You will learn more by listening than by trying to power through to get your message to another listener. At some point your conversation partner will run down and when you do speak your listeners will recognize that they have been heard.

3. *Don't lose your temper.* One of the sorriest sights you will see is a senior who has lost his or her control and let emotions take charge. Hapless (though rarely blameless) subordinates will have to take it, but in the doing they will resent their treatment and some of the senior's message will be lost in the transmission. You don't have to persuade a subordinate, though in most circumstances it is the best result, but you do have to avoid putting impediments in the path of full communication.

4. *Watch your body language.* Your manner of listening may convey impatience, scorn, or disagreement before your conversation partner has been fully heard. The way you listen can be just as damaging as the words you speak.

5. *Combine candor with tact.* You are listening and speaking not to whitewash, agree for the sake of agreeing, or to make your audience feel good. There should be messages being transmitted and received, messages with real content. Often it will be necessary to risk offense to make the point. But needless offensiveness should be avoided. You are not a salesman but don't make yourself the enemy either.

6. *Observe the art of administering and receiving a "chewing out."* Sometimes your subordinates—or you—will richly deserve a tongue-lashing (which some call "counseling") for a lapse of judgment. Your state of mind for each role is important. Anger or resentment get in the way of resolution. During your career you will observe masters of the art of administering a reprimand—and less obviously the conduct of those who take the rebuke to heart and respond positively to one of the painful if necessary rites of passage in a naval career. Occasionally, when on the receiving end you may feel an injustice has been done. Learn from it for the time when you will be on the other end. *Never complain, never explain. Learn instead.*

7. *Make the effort to learn the art of conversation.* You may be shy or

you may want only to talk shop. You have to learn to open up and expand your horizons. Talking shop works in some settings and is a social drag in others. In most cases you have left half of your audience out of the flow (e.g., spouses and non-naval friends). Observe how good conversationalists operate. Select, pursue, or join in a theme that includes others and is not the subject of one's own monologue. Good conversationalists are keenly aware of when they are talking too much and make a conscious effort to include others ("What do you think, Tom?"). The themes can be commonplace but of wide interest. While a discussion of the weather is a last resort, there are other subjects less banal and of wider interest (the headlines in the morning paper, a new restaurant in town). It is easy for such conversation to spill over into gossip, a lapse in manners that should be anticipated and avoided.

8. *Treat all your associates as ladies and gentlemen—even if they are not.* If you find yourself tailoring your language or demeanor to fit your perception of your audience, welcome back to the world of bad manners. That does not mean that you address your division the same way you address your commanding officer but it does mean you are to focus on communicating with each member of your audience with due respect.

9. *Go out of your way to introduce yourself to those you don't know.* This does not mean thrusting yourself on the unwilling, but it suggests a sensitivity to including strangers. Nothing bothers a host or hostess more than to have a stand-offish guest who doesn't uphold their part of the social bargain and becomes a problem on a dinner party seating chart.

10. *Cultivate an ability to laugh at yourself.* You will notice that some of your contemporaries particularly enjoy pointing out the foibles of others and make others the butt of their humor. If you find that your humor is mostly at the expense of others and you take yourself too seriously, you are becoming a social handicap. Among the

first results will be a reduction in the number of your close friends and a wariness in befriending you.

Manners at Official Functions

I have in mind such occasions as a change of command ceremony and the inevitable subsequent reception, a hail and farewell party, a ship launching or commissioning, or a reception for an honored guest. *If there is a receiving line it is your duty to go through it except in the most pressing emergency.* In that case you owe it to the honoree to express your regrets and pass along your respects at the first subsequent opportunity.

I have observed some officers who see a change of command ceremony as an opportunity to grind axes with attending seniors, "press the flesh" and talk shop with contemporaries, or otherwise "make their number" (ensure their presence is noted). Often lost in passing is the welcoming and saying farewell to the new and old skippers and their families in attendance. You were not invited to the ceremony and the reception in order to follow your own agenda and at your convenience. You were invited to witness an important rite of passage and to help lend dignity to the occasion. Don't abuse that trust.

Entertaining

What is the object of entertaining in a Navy setting? What does it contribute to the unit's mission and to becoming a better naval officer? Isn't it overdone? Isn't it a little too structured, and perhaps akin to the Kabuki dance so prominent in the Japanese culture? If it were so important, why doesn't the government defray the costs? And so on. All good questions, though some are a bit naïve. To put it simply most Navy entertaining is intended to foster good relations among shipmates who may go to battle together and with their families whose support is so vital to good unit morale. It does this by providing an alternative to the workplace setting where informal conversation can be conducted and whereby seniors and their juniors can get to know their shipmates better than in the official atmosphere aboard ship or at the office.

For example, if you are a junior officer on an aircraft carrier, a large amphibious ship, or a tender you will rarely have an opportunity to converse with your commanding officer outside of a social setting. Yet your skipper is signing a fitness report on your performance that will have a great influence on your future. That officer owes it to you and you owe it to them to provide and attend functions where this greater knowledge can be gained and shared. In smaller wardrooms or offices where the skipper gets to know each of his juniors, this function is important for an additional reason: you are so few in number that each member bears a significantly larger percentage of the unit's workload. It is vital that each comes to know well the character, style, and preferences of the other to maximize unit effectiveness. In a larger unit a single defective part (or member) is less critical to the performance of the whole because there is backup available.

In responding to the gibe that if entertaining were so mission essential the Navy would defray the costs involved, two points need to be made. First, the government does defray in part the costs of official entertaining by high officials for the simple reason that it is so important and it is recognized as such even by most bean counters on Congressional staffs and in the Pentagon. Second, I think the last thing most skippers would want would be to have to structure their guest lists to fit some official-necessity criterion. They entertain because they enjoy it and see the need for it. Moreover, they were entertained on the way up and feel some need to reciprocate courtesies to the new generation of officers.

Thus Navy entertaining, to the degree it raises greater awareness and generates esprit de corps, does enhance unit effectiveness in largely intangible but nonetheless important dimensions. Is it too structured? Perhaps, if it becomes automatic or expected and if seniors don't exert themselves to liven it up. Some seniors and their spouses find it difficult to unbend in a social setting—see the ten social commandments at the beginning of this chapter. But there is no need to fall into a rut. If you are a junior officer and are tasked to organize the next ship, squadron, or office party, let your imagination take wing. You may see some adjustments made by your boss, but get out in front and innovate if you can.

I know a skipper who successfully broke the social mold by hosting in his ship a reception and dinner (fitted to the environment of the modern Navy) of "an evening with Jack Aubrey," the hero of Patrick O'Brian's novels and of the popular movie *Master and Commander*. Many old traditions rarely observed today were demonstrated by the ship's company and the guests. To my knowledge such an entertainment had not been conducted before and it was a great success and the talk of the waterfront for weeks thereafter.

As a junior officer you will find yourself entertained by others at their home or at cocktail or dinner parties elsewhere. It is often difficult to fully reciprocate, particularly if you are not married or are away from your home port. An obligation to reciprocate is created but the opportunity may not be available and that handicap is well understood by old Navy hands and their spouses. Don't worry about the circumstance but be alert to an opportunity to discharge your obligation in the future— sometimes perhaps years later. A simple appreciative note to the hostess is an adequate placeholder in the interim.

I found that I could often repay my social obligations to former seniors long retired and that their inclusion was much appreciated by all concerned. What is needed is a level of sensitivity to what we owe others and amnesia about what others may owe us. For you junior officers, you overlook the social connection of Navy life at your peril. I have known junior officers who never went to a command social function— not even to those hosted by their contemporaries. Most were shy or considered other diversions more interesting or more important. Their inward-looking mind-set and lack of consideration of their obligations will not only deny them a long-term source of pleasure but will also over the years become an immense professional handicap.

15

Are You Still Learning?

A man can always find a chance for doing nothing as amply
and with as ecstatic a satisfaction as the world allows.
—Hilaire Belloc[1]

This chapter is not about going back to school. It is about stretching
yourself professionally—just as you would in aerobic, strength, or range
of motion exercises. Are you in a mental rut or are you keeping your
mind nimble by confronting new challenges? These challenges may be
internal—setting goals, working to achieve them, learning new skills,
doing what you hate to do but doing it well anyway. It is easy to fall into
a rut in a career, perhaps especially a naval career. We are trained to follow procedures, some of them written in blood. We stand watches, we
conduct preflights of our aircraft, we take routine exams such as rules
of the nautical road, NATOPS for aviators, physical fitness tests, and so
on. For many of us there is a temptation to go into automatic in the face
of such routine.

But many officers pride themselves as innovators and set goals that
go beyond the professional parameters—a perfect score on a written
exam, learning something new each watch, learning something new on
each flight, adding a new wrinkle to a time-honored routine. In this
chapter we cover some items that warrant your special attention as you
seek to improve your professional performance.

Public Speaking

I know officers who run the other way when asked to speak at a public gathering or command function. The excuses are many and rarely good. Public speaking is a tool that must be honed and used. Others rely on a written script or almost as bad, crib notes. You must discipline yourself to fix in your mind what you want to say—a simple expandable outline. You can practice in the privacy of your office to see how well you have it down, but come "game day" you must mount the rostrum and "knock 'em dead."

Public oratory is a double-edged sword. If you are or become a good oral communicator, you will find that it will speed you on your way to career success. Alternatively, it can be a dragging anchor on your career if you lack those skills. As you progress in your career, you will find that your oral communication skills become even more important. I use the term "public speaking" to include more than addressing a group from a lectern or delivering a speech to the local chamber of commerce or a gathering of fellow alumni. Your skills—or lack thereof—will be on open display in your first job as a junior officer as you speak to your Sailors or to the wardroom on some professional subject. You cannot hide your skills or deficiencies. You either go with what you have or you make what you have better.

You can listen to a good speaker and tell immediately whether or not there is an organized mind at work and whether the speaker knows how to capture the audience's attention and keep it. This book is not a primer on speaking in public; there are many such and most are good. It helps to see what they have to say, but the really important fact is that to be good takes practice. Do not shrink from a tasking that involves speaking to others. You don't have to grab for the mike but you should be up to the occasions when they occur.

We have space enough to forward a few tips on speaking that have served naval officers well through the ages.

1. *Know the subject matter* you are talking about. An uninformed briefer or one with large gaps in his or her background will lose the audience. Winging it is not the same as not knowing your stuff.

2. *Speak so your audience can hear you.* If necessary work on your speaking voice. It should be firm, vigorous, direct, and convincing. This will come with practice. Mumblers and whisperers need not apply. Shouters or sermonizers are not needed either.

3. *Put yourself in your audience's chairs.* Don't speak down to them, look at every one of them as you deliver your message. Don't offer apologies or excuses; no one wants to hear them. Make eye contact with every part of the audience.

4. If time permits, *organize your thoughts into a logical progression.* Good writing skills will help you here.

5. *Observe good speakers* and analyze why they succeeded.

6. *Keep it short*—but cover the subject assigned.

7. A talk *delivered without notes* is ten times better than one delivered using notes; a talk delivered using notes is ten times better than one delivered using a script that is read to the audience.

8. *Use uncontrived humor.* It establishes a bond with the audience on even the driest subjects.

9. Recognize that *most audiences are on your side*; they want you to succeed.

10. *Practice, practice, practice!*

11. *As you become more senior and a part of some gathering, ask yourself what you would say to the assembled multitude.*[2]

Writing

More communications! You will find that being a naval officer means dealing with seniors and subordinates and that the better you communicate, the better officer you will be. Communicating is a close second to being a pro. You may know your stuff, but if you can't communicate information to your Sailors or prepare official documents (e.g., performance evaluations for your Sailors), few will know you are a pro.

Some officers are good speakers and others are good writers. Most of the time the two go together. Why? Because both require knowing the subject matter and the ability to organize ideas and present them in a logical, complete, and understandable order. Good logical thinking makes writing and speaking much easier. You may be able to entertain without logical thinking skills, but you cannot *inform* without them except perhaps at the pep talk level. Logical thinking starts with that hated topic—freshman English composition. Your English teacher had it right. If you can't put a sentence together, you can't put a paragraph together, and you will not be as good a speaker or writer as you could be. Like speaking, writing takes practice.

Start small. Concentrate on composing well-written evaluations on your Sailors. Put yourself in the shoes of those who will be reading the finished report. Then go on to writing a good summary input to your fitness report. Summarize your division's accomplishments, your efforts at self-improvement, and your objectives. Root around in your department and find out what reports and summaries are needed by your chain of command and start practicing your writing by attempting to improve them—clarity, brevity, organization. Train yourself to think—and speak—in complete sentences. I guarantee your boss needs all the help you can offer. If you want to get favorable notice in your organization there are few ways better than having a way with words *to communicate.*

Professional Reading

In my earlier book on naval officer performance I emphasized the need to keep up to date on your profession by reading daily.[3] For example, such magazines as the U.S. Naval Institute *Proceedings*—read it cover to cover over the period of a week or two. As you get more senior there are others that will come to your notice: the *Naval War College Review,* the *Joint Forces*

Quarterly, Foreign Affairs, Sea Power, and many others. Keep a book handy for reading on trips. Lighten up by reading fiction on a variety of subjects. I offer a few more thoughts on professional reading in appendix D.

Flexing Your Mind

It is not enough to take in information (as in reading) and put it out in writing and speeches. You need to cultivate the ability to think analytically, with flexibility (questioning assumptions—in your mind, not by becoming a pain to others—at least not yet), agility in applying knowledge to concrete situations, and exercising your imagination in the professional sphere. This is the hardest of skills to impart to others and to learn. It takes professional curiosity, playing "what if" games with yourself and others as the occasion presents itself, and not being satisfied with the pat answer. It means questioning glib judgments such as:

- "I'd rather be right than. . . ." (Why not both?)
- "It's been tried before and. . . ." (Were the circumstances the same in both cases?)
- "It can't be done." (Has it been tried? Where? When?)
- "Never volunteer." (Would you rather be ordered to do something, or get out ahead of the problem?)
- "The only legitimate answers to a senior's question or order are: yes sir, no sir, aye aye sir, or I'll find out sir." (Does this useful midshipman's guide apply equally to a commissioned officer that is communicating with his or her senior?)
- "There is no difference between loyalty and integrity; they are different sides of the same coin." (How far do you carry loyalty to an *individual* before integrity is compromised?)
- "Success in the Navy depends on who you know." (Does it depend at all on *what* you know? Do service politics win battles? How do you explain the Navy's great victories?)

- "Metaphors are for simple minds." (Metaphors and their testing for accuracy and relevance is one of the major tools of the imaginative mind.)

The possibilities for similar mental games are infinite and limited only by your imagination. There are limits on how you can *act* imaginatively but there are no limits that keep you from *thinking* imaginatively. For example, superimpose paradigms for other activities on those at hand. Examine analogues and metaphors for their weaknesses and applicability. The sports and business metaphors are overworked in American society (e.g., keep your eye on the ball, all that counts is the bottom line). Are there other fields that could expand our minds if applied to the naval officer's business? What about science, the arts, medicine, classical economics, music?

While on Watch

You will spend much of your career on watch. Are these hours all tedium, or do you have a way to spice them up? Some watches take care of themselves: you are in the midst of demanding tactical evolutions that require you and your watch's complete attention. While a task group is proceeding from point to point, the officer in tactical command has a set of drills to keep the watch—signal bridge, combat, weapons stations—"entertained" and alert. But there are numerous other times, some of long duration, when there is nothing but the routine of watch standing to contend with. As officer of the deck or engineering officer of the watch, you could use this time to test and exercise the watch. Task your junior officer of the deck or other watch subordinate to come up with a drill or a test of knowledge on which all watch standers must concentrate. Emergency drills are a good place to start. Ask why some evolutions are necessary as part of a response to an emergency. *Learn something new and teach something new on every watch.* Some will hate to see a lethargic routine disturbed, but most will enter into the spirit of the game and be better Sailors for it.

16

What Is Your Competitive Edge?

So cheer up, my son. Play the game. Take your medicine. Don't squeal. Watch your step. After all, it is a splendid profession and an honorable career.

—Capt. A. P. Niblack, advice to his son[1]

By now it is obvious to you that your rise in the naval profession is a competitive business. The essence of screening and promotion boards is to find the *best* fitted for success in the Navy of today and tomorrow. Many who are able and qualified will be defeated by the numbers involved. All may be good but not all can be the best. You may be good enough to run and finish the race but tangible honors go to those who finish first or close to it. It is time to look inward on what you bring to the race, not look outward to how others are doing.

First, you should catalog your strengths and then go on to your weaknesses. This exercise will tell you what assignments offer the best opportunity to contribute to the Navy's mission and to your own success in its pursuit. This self-examination is critically important both to your progress and putting in place a plan of action to remedy any shortcomings. You simply cannot afford to go through a naval career serving in assignments that fit your weaknesses better than your strengths. To navigate successfully you need to know both the hazards to navigation and your best points of sailing.

To some it is difficult to acknowledge any weaknesses—even in private. To acknowledge weakness is seen as the next step to timidity and failure to act—both well outside the naval tradition. Yet we all have weaknesses in one form or another. You may be a superb ship handler but a terrible administrator. You may be a good tactician but a poor planner. You may be a good hands-on leader of Sailors, but a poor student in an academic setting. You may a good physical specimen and in good condition, but all thumbs when it comes to briefing your boss. You may have kissed the blarney stone but can't write a good staff paper or estimate of the situation. You get the idea. If you know where you fall on the performance scale among these standards you can exploit your strengths and compensate for and correct your weaknesses. But it starts and ends with knowing yourself—and whether or not you have the will and are ready to make the sacrifices entailed in improvement. I can promise you one thing: if you have weaknesses the naval environment will discover them sooner or later.

Taking Inventory

First we need to examine the skill sets that define a top performing naval officer over a full career, not just as a hot shot junior officer. Earlier chapters in this book have foreshadowed some of these parameters. As you review the skills set out below bear in mind that their relative importance changes over the years of your career and as you climb the promotion ladder. For now we are seeking coverage of the most relevant and those with the highest leverage. This may seem like a tedious, bean-counting exercise, but it has major implications not only for complete and realistic self-evaluation but also for helping you foresee what lies ahead and preparing yourself for it. So, roll up your sleeves and plow through it with me. When we are done, we will establish a perspective that will give you a road map through the essential milestones of your career. The listing set out below constitutes the skills needed for success. The first skill is being a pro. Rate yourself on a scale of one to five on each of the following items (five is "excellent" and one is "poor").

I. Being a Pro
   A. Demonstrating a seaman's professional skills
      1. Ship handling
      2. Watch standing
      3. Sea knowledge or "sea sense" (e.g., weather, ground tackle, boats, replenishment at sea)
      4. Ship knowledge (e.g., engineering plant, damage control, ship handling characteristics, combat systems)
      5. Tactical and maneuvering sense
   B. [For airmen] Demonstrating an airman's professional skills
      1. Hand-eye coordination
      2. Situational awareness
      3. Air sense (e.g., weather, aerodynamics, carrier systems)
      4. Aircraft knowledge (e.g., systems, procedures, emergencies)
      5. Landing grades (applies to carrier aviators)
      6. Carrier discipline and procedures
      7. Flight crew management
   C. Demonstrating a warrior's professional skills
      1. Effectiveness in operating weapons systems (e.g., targeting, decision making, plant operation, maneuvering)
      2. Ability to integrate diverse systems to maximize total output
      3. Tactical sense (e.g., ability to sense "the moment," to arrive at timely and sound system employment, extract information needed to make winning decisions)
      4. Maintaining and supporting installed systems (e.g., maximizing performance, reducing "down time," managing needed support)

II. Being an Officer
   A. Developing leadership, followership, and problem-solving skills
      1. Leading and motivating Sailors and other officers

    2. Professional zeal (e.g., "can do," readily accepting and discharging responsibilities)

    3. Cooperating with others (e.g., people skills)

    4. Decisiveness, sound judgment, creative imagination

B. Seeing the "big picture"

    1. Suppleness of mind, willingness to innovate, accept the good ideas of others

    2. Studying your bosses and learning from them (e.g., mentally "fleeting up")

    3. Unit mission awareness

    4. Preparing yourself for the next step on the performance ladder

    5. Ability to plan and manage effectively (operations, workload, crew utilization)

C. Communicating

    1. Ability to prepare and effectively deliver a briefing on a complex subject

    2. Ability to write an effective report, staff paper, or essay on naval subjects

    3. The ability to prepare and deliver a motivational, informational, or congratulatory speech in a variety of settings

    4. The ability to address a group of your subordinates, convey important information in a form that they will understand, motivate them to perform assigned tasks, and gain their cooperation

III. Being a Manager

    A. Utilizing resources effectively and efficiently

    B. Ability to relate system payoffs to inputs and their costs

    C. Identifying and solving funding and other resource problems

    D. Effectiveness in administration (e.g., organization, procedures, staffing, ADP systems)

IV. Being a Planner, Student, and Analyst

    A. Ability to integrate system knowledge and environmental knowledge over time

        1. An imaginative approach to analyzing and solving complex problems

        2. An awareness of gaps of information and instituting approaches to fill them

        3. An eye for the important detail and its relation to the whole (i.e., the ability to see the forest and the trees at the same time)

        4. An ability to foresee future effects of current decisions

        5. An ability to assimilate a vast quantity of knowledge, extract what is most needed, and apply it to the problem at hand

    B. An ability to apply theory and abstract knowledge to practical problems

        1. An ability to operate effectively in an academic environment, either as a student or an instructor

        2. A recognition of the limits and leverage of academic knowledge in the solution of "real world" problems

        3. A respect for book knowledge and an understanding of its proper interface with operations and training

V. Being a Staff Officer

    A. A healthy respect for the delineation between command and staff roles

        1. The ability to maintain a dual focus between the responsibilities of a flag and a subordinate unit commanding officer

        2. An ability to bring staff capabilities to bear on the problems faced by commanding officers

        3. An ability to articulate policies and orders such that they

carry out the flag officer's intent while conveying the information in terms that are both understandable and executable by his or her subordinates

B. An ability to integrate missions across command echelons

C. The ability to establish and operate systems that ensure that the flag officer is sufficiently informed to make sound decisions

D. An ability to establish and operate systems that translate the admiral's decisions into orders and thence into action and to monitor the results

This is an imposing list of skills needed in a naval officer. As if that were not enough, there is another dimension to this list—time and seniority. Together, the two dimensions (skills and seniority) form a matrix of needed skills at each stage of your career. Many of the cells will be empty because there has been no opportunity to fill them. If you are a junior officer there will be more empty ones than filled. Not all skills are applicable to every step of your career progression. Moreover the specific content of each skill will change as you advance to more senior billets. Some readers will note the omission of an important skill. By all means add it to your personal listing.

You should by now perceive a personal road map emerging from this exercise. Skills you need are more visible, skills areas where you are weak (or simply haven't had an opportunity to acquire) start to jump out at you and suggest remedial or planning action. You will probably never be able to fill all the cells, but you will at least know what the "perfect naval officer's sea bag" looks like.

We are not done with this matrix yet. How would you score yourself now for each of the skill categories appropriate to your current stage in your naval career? How about the next stage—perhaps as a department head if you are now a division officer, or as a commanding officer if you are now a department head, and on up the ladder?

As you look at the skill set in each cell of the matrix, your weaknesses or strengths, either current or prospective, will be apparent to you. Rigorous candor and thoroughness are needed to "grade" yourself. Self-delusion or cursory examination will return to bite you at a later date if you are less than candid or complete in your appraisal. As you go about this arduous and somewhat unpleasant task, ask yourself what tangible evidence of each cell can be cited in your behalf.

A Perspective on the Naval Skill Set

As a midshipman or junior officer you should be focused on the "being a pro" and "being an officer" skill sets *as they apply to a junior officer.* Your department head and skipper will have commensurate skills associated with their career points. Their needed skills are similar but qualitatively different. The last three skill sets are more oriented to your seniors in the grade of commander, captain, and flag. You should be aware of the requirements that lie ahead of you and seize opportunities that come your way in order to meet them.

Earlier in this book we observed that a career was built block by block to attain top performance. You should be looking at the skill set matrix horizontally as well as vertically. For example, you are building on your naval officer skills as you look forward to the next step in your professional growth. But you also need to look vertically to see what new skills you will have to acquire and exercise. For example, a department head aboard ship is not only looking horizontally at the contents of the commanding officer's "being a pro" cell but is also looking vertically at the "being a staff officer" cell to acquire new skills.

The skills matrix can also be used to identify cases of career stagnation. Some officers progress little beyond the department head column and limit themselves to "being a pro" skills for their billet without making the leap to the adjacent cell or putting new cells in their sea bag. Some officers are so capable and so active that, while doing their current job well, they are leaping ahead to start furnishing the next or other cells in the matrix. The real naval pros keep the whole matrix in view and have firm views as to which cells are most important, particularly those most intimately related to command at sea.

But a myopic focus on duty at sea does not encompass an entire career. As you become more senior a greater portion of your time will be spent ashore and, in a seeming paradox, how well you perform in important billets ashore plays a major role in determining your promotability. Alas, the Navy is more than driving ships and flying airplanes. You are correct to focus on the path to command at sea but at higher ranks good sea skills will be taken as a given; if you don't have them, you aren't in the ball game. However, selection and screening boards will ask what else you bring to the party. This is particularly important in screening for major command where the pool from which future flag officers are chosen is formed.

Therefore don't dismiss the "being a manager," or "being a staff officer" boxes too quickly as not being important way stations on the route to command. The Navy's top leadership wants its key leaders to be seasoned and "hot runners" at sea *and* capable in running the Navy shore establishment. It won't surprise you to learn that this business is one of timing and progression and top performance to be a competitor. Some will say it is luck rather than planning. There is some luck in any human enterprise, but to say that it is decisive is to surrender the initiative to events—very bad advice for any naval officer.

Your Edge

You have gone through the inventory of skills needed and located where you are in it. You have gone on to grade yourself in the appropriate cells of the matrix. You have identified strengths and weaknesses and projected ahead in time and seniority to the next column of cells. You know where you must improve and you know where your strengths are. You have confirmed that you are a good seaman or airman and that you lead

Sailors fairly well. However, you also are coming to realize that you are not a great communicator. Briefings and writing papers for the skipper are a real pain and you aren't *yet* very good at them. But you think you have potential as a planner, student, or analyst. On the other hand you hate the kind of challenges inherent in management of resources. Perhaps if you can buff up your communications skills, you have a future as a planner or a staff officer. Perhaps your biggest edge will be that you systematically have looked at your career—past, present, and future—and plotted your own course to your objectives.

17

Opportunities, Disappointments, and Injustices

> He had reached a solstice in his life, one of those dead points
> when one requires some foreign force in order to avoid
> stagnation.
> —Van Wyck Brooks[1]

Yogi Berra advised, "When you come to a fork in the road, take it." Yogi can't help you in this business! You will find that in your career you sometimes come to a fork in the road where the decision you make will affect everything that follows. For a midshipman, and occasionally as a junior officer, the choice (assuming you have one) involves your selection of a career track such as surface warfare, submarine duty, special operations, or aviation—or some subspecialty within those communities. Or later as a junior officer ending your first sea tour, when you are confronted with the choice of graduate work or instructor duty. As you get more senior, you may face the choice of working for (and learning from) a truly superb naval officer who is a "comer" as we discussed earlier, or staying on the track to the next billet in your progression to command. Or in another crossroads you may face the choice between gaining a valued "credential" (e.g., an MBA) or gaining important experience needed to fit you for eventual command. Your detailer may even ask how you feel about extending for a year in your current command, another possible fork in the road. And as you become even more senior you will face the choice of leaving or staying in the service.

It will not surprise you that there is no one-size-fits-all answer to these questions—particularly when you add on some important family considerations omitted from this listing. Your problem usually centers on both objectives (strategy) and how to maximize the payoff of the decision (tactics). The systems analysts have a name for analysis of this kind: multivariant decision analysis. Don't worry, we aren't going to load that on you! But a key ingredient of such analysis as applied to your career is knowing what your objectives are and rank ordering them as they apply to the decision at hand.

Your Objectives

Let us assume you are happily married, have a spouse working outside the home, have healthy children, are finishing your department head tour and have done well, have managed to pick up an engineering degree on your last shore tour, and are faced with a key choice as you start to look at your second shore tour. Your objectives might look like this (you do the rank ordering):

- The welfare of my family (e.g., education, health, stability)
- Staying on the path to eventual command (e.g., stay near my warfare specialty)
- Enhancing my professional development (e.g., pick up an additional professional skill in high demand)
- Serving in billets I enjoy (e.g., I can contribute and the tour will help me stay on track)

Although not of immediate concern, you realize that there are at least three other objectives out there in the distance.

- Keeping my hat in the ring for eventual consideration for high rank (e.g., serving in a joint or combined billet, attending a war college course, or professional military education)

- Working for the best officers in the service (to learn and to prosper)
- Preparing for the day when I must or should leave the service and reenter civilian life

If this is not a complete list for you, add your own entries (e.g., your spouse's career opportunities and development; or less seriously, a fur-lined billet in Hawaii or the United Kingdom). You get the idea how open-ended this whole subject is. And you realize that as each objective is added to the pile, analyzing them, one against the other, becomes much more complicated. But at least you have made a start: you have it out in the open where you and your spouse can examine it, tweak it, and get some sense of possible rank ordering and what possible future assignments (and possibly personal sacrifices) lie behind each objective. You should also get a sense of what is important now and what may become important later.

You have done your homework—and now your detailer (or a chance opportunity) enters the picture. You have been told that it is time to pay the piper and take your overseas tour. Or, the detailer has informed you that even though your postgraduate course was in engineering (and you believed a payback tour in a systems command would be the result), you are being considered for assignment to a seagoing staff headed by a hard-charging admiral who is well known in the service and that some say will be a future CNO.

Such assignment, however, will mean extending your sea duty and delaying assignment to Washington or to one of the junior courses at a war or staff college. The sea staff assignment means that you will be away from home a lot but that your family will stay in your current home-port complex. Add to that your spouse has been offered a promotion if he or she will move to Washington or Jacksonville. See how complex it all becomes?

I cannot give you a map through this maze. The best I can do is help you examine your own objectives and your (and your family's) priorities. In the examples cited there are trade-offs as you are well aware. It is time to get them down on paper—assuming the Naval Personnel Command has not already taken the choice out of your hands. When Pasteur said, "Chance favors the prepared mind," he may have had you in mind in preparing for the inevitable dilemmas of a naval career. Oh, by the way, the tempo and stakes get higher as you become more senior!

Trifectas

Sometimes there are opportunities to kill more than one bird with a single stone (assignment). You already realize that at some point you will have a Washington tour (most of the time more than one or two), an overseas tour, a war college tour, a joint duty tour, a command tour, and so on. Have you considered the possibilities of doubling— or even tripling—up?

For example, why not combine your overseas and joint/combined tour in a single tour? How about a joint or combined staff located overseas (e.g., Japan, Korea, Southwest Asia, NATO) or a joint staff tour in Washington, D.C.? How about a command or stepping-stone prior tour overseas (the numerous fleet units stationed in Japan come to mind)? Although not likely to count as an overseas tour, consider that assignment as a student at an allied war college overseas may be helpful in putting off—perhaps entirely—the need to serve later in a billet overseas. A short follow-on tour as a member of the staff of the college may meet overseas duty criteria. Your fertile mind may conceive of other combinations. A rare trifecta at one time might have been a command tour as skipper of one of NATO's Standing Naval Force ships. The idea is not to be cute, but to double up when you can because there is only so much time to do all that is expected of you as you proceed from assignment to assignment. My personal favorites are: a command (or a preparatory department head) tour in a unit based in Japan, duty on the Joint Staff of the JCS in Washington, or on an overseas joint or combined staff. I managed only the last of the three in my own career.

Bonus Commands

These are additional command opportunities that fall only to the fortunate and able few. For example, some junior surface warriors have an opportunity to get command as a lieutenant or lieutenant commander (e.g., mine sweeper, other small combatants) and later get their commander command (e.g., a destroyer or amphib). Some aviators can follow a successful sea command with a tour in command of a corresponding fleet replacement squadron ashore. But these days most officers will only have two sea commands before reaching flag: a command in the rank of commander and a major command in the rank of captain. When I was growing up in the Navy I knew officers who had held as many as six commands at sea—before reaching flag rank. Those days appear to be gone forever. But you may find yourself going from one command to another (as I did twice). Moreover, you might be ripped out to fill in as a stopgap. If you get these extra commands, count your blessings even if they involve some personal inconvenience.

Time for a sea story. The son of a good friend of mine was looking forward to returning to sea duty and a major command. He had been screened and was awaiting orders. It happened that he became aware that a shore command billet was opening up and that detailers were hard pressed to fill it because of its location. It was an overseas shore station on the major command list. The young captain seized on the opportunity and offered to accept the overseas shore command if he were guaranteed his major command at sea after successful completion of the overseas shore command tour. Expediency faced by the warfare community manager in the Naval Personnel Command and creative opportunism exercised by this officer resulted in his getting two back-to-back major commands, one ashore and the other afloat. The story is still unfolding but I wouldn't be surprised to see his name on a flag list in the next couple of years.

Career Disappointments

Some possibilities are obvious: failure to screen for command or failure to be selected for promotion. Other disappointments might include going late to command or getting a command at a low point in its deployment cycle. Or your sea command is in a ship or squadron type that was low on your preference list. Or you could have screened for command and subsequently been "de-screened" either because of your comparative performance or more likely because the number of commands available has decreased. Earlier in your career you may have been put into a warfare pipeline that was far from your first choice but the "needs of the service" prevailed over your preferences. Or you may have been ordered to an overseas tour and because of family needs you had to go unaccompanied.

I have never met a successful naval officer (including most flag officers) who at some time had not experienced a seemingly significant career disappointment, a disappointment that at the time loomed very large in seeming to prejudice future career prospects. You may have experienced some of it already in your career—but there is more ahead. And not just in a naval career. The ability to bounce back, "power through it," persevere, and not become discouraged will see you through more than career disappointments. These attributes will also see you through combat and peacetime stress alike.

There is little that I can say in this book that will help you during these downturns. It is enough that you are warned that they will occur and that you are not being singled out. They happen to everyone—though many will keep their disappointment to themselves. Not a very bright prospect, you may say. But what more than balances the low points are the many high points that you will experience. A final piece of advice: Resist the temptation to blame someone else or the system for your misfortune. The temptation will be strong, but put it aside. Your own self-respect and the respect of others demand it. You didn't make the playing field, you didn't referee the game, and you didn't pick the competition, but you chose to play the game. It is demeaning to envy or denigrate those who also played and won. Or to lay it all at the doorstep of lady luck.

In my view the quiet courage, resolution, and acceptance of responsibility of those who have "lost," missed a hurdle, or suffered a setback is one of the glories of the naval service right up there beside the accolades conferred on the victors, the winners, and in some cases the more fortunate. Early in your career, promise yourself that you will not be a sore loser and that you will take full responsibility not only for your successes but also your disappointments.

This is a good point to bring up a possibility that might have occurred to you already. You may already know that you don't want to compete for, or you know yourself well enough to know that you are not and will not be a competitor in rising to, flag rank. One premise of this book and its predecessor is that some if not most readers are interested in taking the next step in a naval career and that at the end of a succession of such steps lies flag rank. Many successful naval officers—success is measured in many ways—find their niche in the ranks of commander and captain. It is there they can contribute and enjoy the benefits of a full and rewarding career. They don't ask to run the outfit; they just want to be a respected and productive part of it. These officers are the treasures of the naval service. I served with many of them and remain in their debt for their example of loyal, selfless, and effective service.

The Ability to Adapt

Despite the structured nature of the naval environment you will encounter situations that test your adaptability: working for an idiosyncratic commanding officer, a job for which you are ill-prepared, the unexpected and unwanted fast set of orders from the Naval Personnel Command, a temporary duty assignment involving great personal and family hardship, being replaced in a good job by someone who happens to be senior to you, being assigned an onerous and time-consuming collateral duty, and so on.

Your stock in trade as an officer, particularly an unrestricted line officer, is the ability to adapt to change and do so effectively. Line officers over the years have taken great pride in being able to complete any assigned task and doing so with some dash and professionalism. A common boast was, "Any line officer can do that—just part of a day's work."

Injustices Large and Small

There will come a time in your naval career—I would add *any* career—when you will believe an injustice has been done to you. In some cases they coincide with disappointments. But there are also the trivial injustices—it wasn't your fault—when you are held responsible for another's shortcomings. Here I am not talking about the shortcomings of your subordinates; that, after all, is your responsibility as the person in charge. No, here I am talking about a mistake made by a third party or the quirkiness of a senior that puts you in the position of taking undeserved blame.

A sea story on a trivial matter that may make the point. I was once attached to an antisubmarine squadron on an aircraft carrier. We were out looking for a Soviet submarine in the middle of the Atlantic. It was a nasty rainy summer night and I was the last of the flight to land aboard. As I climbed out of my aircraft, the flight deck officer approached me and told me the admiral wanted to see me right away.

I had no inkling of the reason for this order but proceeded immediately to the flag bridge. At the door to flag plot I was met by the staff watch officer (wearing service dress blue and with his binoculars around his neck as his badge of office). He informed me that I could not enter flag plot or the flag bridge in my flight gear (it was a warm night and my flight suit was sweat-streaked). I pointed out that the admiral wanted to see me. He responded that it didn't matter and directed me to go down and get in proper attire.

Some twenty minutes later freshly showered and wearing a full uniform I presented myself on the flag bridge. In a gruff voice the admiral's first question was, "What took you so long?" This was followed by a short lecture on punctuality and his need for immediate information from aircrews that were aloft. What would you have done in this situation? Tell the admiral you were told to report immediately by one officer and turned away at the door to flag plot by another? Or that a quick shower and a pressed uniform stood between him and the prompt delivery of the needed information? John Masters's advice, "Never complain, never explain," comes to mind.

Sometimes doing your duty and common sense will get you cross-threaded with a senior who does not know all the circumstances. You were there and you had to make the decision for good or ill. If you start worrying about what your boss will think when you must make a prompt decision, or if you blindly follow orders in the belief your boss will get you out of trouble if you follow them, or if you plot the safe course when boldness is needed, you are settling for safety at the expense of doing your duty.

No officer can be effective if he or she is always looking over his or her shoulder or at the grandstands to see what others think. Sometimes the result is injustice. And yes it is your boss's duty to know the circumstances before holding you fully accountable. But bosses are human too (you already know that you are). Learn to accept life's injustices—large or small—as part of the playing field and not fret because you were not fairly treated.

18

Your Command Tour

From the moment you, as the new skipper, step aboard you are
on trial before your officers and men. Responsibility for the
ship as well as for the men is yours.
—Capt. Harley F. Cope[1]

In this chapter I am talking principally about a sea command tour in the
grade of commander. Some able few will get the plum of an earlier command (particularly surface warfare officers because there are more junior commands in that warfare community), but command in the grade
of commander is your goal. For some it will be their only command.
Major command in the grade of captain comes later and to relatively few.
Just as battalion command is the key intermediate objective for Army and
Marine officers in the grade of lieutenant colonel, command of a ship or
air squadron is the goal for the unrestricted line Navy commander. This
command is where all the threads of your professional voyage come
together.

The path to such command was covered in my earlier book on naval
officer performance and suggested in outline by the earlier chapters in this
book. That path varies by warfare community. In this chapter you will not
find a primer on how to be an outstanding commanding officer. There are
books that specialize in the subject and an entire professional literature
exists on the art and science of military command.[2] What you have read
so far in this book foreshadows the particular challenge of command. You
still must lead subordinates, you still must be professionally competent,

and you still must ensure that your boss (e.g., commodore or air wing commander) gets all your help in meeting his or her mission.

In this chapter we focus on what a good solid command tour means in your overall career development and in preparing you for higher responsibilities. A command tour tests you in adversity and success, in managing and leading, in tactical decision making and seamanship or airmanship, and in understanding the Navy's business. You will find that the good things you previously took for granted are the result of hard work—by someone—and that your role is putting people, machinery, and good decision making together to make those good things happen. You will find yourself stretching to reach a higher level of performance because a large number of people are depending on you—your Sailors and your bosses. When you are done and finally turn over command to your relief, you will do so with a mixture of regret and relief—relief to be leaving behind the pressure to perform at a higher level than you would have thought possible before assuming command. You will find that future promotion and screening boards will be intensely interested in your command tour: what you did, how the command was employed, and how well your boss evaluated your performance. The competition continues. You will be measured with and against your brother and sister skippers, using an absolute standard of failure or success, and even against your predecessors as your reporting senior or selection board members recall their own days in an equivalent command.

Your detailer will also be keenly interested in how you are performing or have performed in command. Just being ordered to command indicates that you are on the first team. Performing well on that team means you are destined for more challenging jobs. You will find that as a skipper, or as a post-command officer, many people are sizing you up and assessing your future. Some commands insist on and deserve (two different things) post-command commanders for key staff jobs. One informed observer has noted that good command performance at sea can outweigh almost all other factors when you are being asked for or

The wise commanding officer takes every opportunity to communicate with members of the unit's crew, including its most junior members, as shown here. *U.S. Naval Institute Photo Archives*

considered for future assignment.[3] A solid sea command tour can outweigh any lack of postgraduate education, service in important staff assignments or Washington duty, or even being less well-known by service reputation.

Why this myopic focus on command, and the performance that justifies such assignment, as the sine qua non of a naval career? The simple answer is because as a skipper there is no place to hide, no one else to blame, and few to help you—it all depends on your professional competence, your will, your courage, and your dedication to your mission. You may have a successful career and rise to the rank of commander but unless you have proved yourself in command, you have not confronted and passed the highest test the Navy uses as a yardstick. Good skippers take a quiet pride in the job—some even glory in it—and take their relief as a demotion. They enjoy the challenges, the excitement, the hands-on work of their profession. Most like their people—Sailors and officers—and work hard to make them better and proud of their job and command. And when it is all over most of them will deserve the title of shipmate and friend.

Many a successful mentorship has been the result of performing well for a skipper who respected your performance. The same goes as well for air wing commanders and commodores who particularly respect your performance in command. To successfully complete your command as a commander is to become a marked man or woman before screening and promotion boards and the people who make the Navy's personnel assignments.

Your Brother and Sister Commanding Officers

Your air wing commander, commodore, or admiral has called a commanding officers conference; there will be many such in your career. You look around the table and you see your contemporaries, all successful in their profession. They had to strive just as hard on the way up as you did to sit at this table. The fact of the matter is that they are your competitors, but only in the context of future promotion and screening boards. For now each of you is a member of a Nelsonian band of brothers. Your boss if he or she is a good one—and most are—will strive to create an atmosphere of working together smoothly in a common cause and just occasionally introducing a whiff of competition. But he or she is very careful not to overdo the latter.

A sea story. Once while I was in command I worked for a very ambitious flag officer, one who was feared, respected mainly for his warfare competence, and heartily disliked by his subordinates. In many cases his first response to sub-caliber performance was to have the offender relieved of duty. This flag officer seemed to delight in calling a conference and then needling some of his commanding officers as to why one of their colleagues always seemed to do a particular evolution better than the others did. When this needling was done in the context of a luncheon in the flag mess, the wry observation of most attending skippers was, "Not what—but who—was on the menu."

The result of this flag officer's penchant for fostering an all-out competition among his subordinates was to poison the wells of professional cooperation in his command. Skippers more closely guarded their secrets of success or failure where previously they were shared for the common good. The level of suspicion among skippers was raised and some became more afraid of being fired peremptorily than of performing well and selflessly. Relations of the skippers with the admiral's staff became strained and the channels of information flow clogged.

While you have no desire to be such a skipper or such a flag officer, there is a nugget of wisdom in this story to guide you in your conduct with your fellow skippers and your bosses. You have it in your power to set an example of cooperation and comradeship with your fellow skippers. It goes without saying that you must avoid "doing handstands" before them for the boss's benefit. Your peers will be quick to notice. By your demeanor and willingness to be a good teammate you will secure the respect of all. All this requires great sensitivity, care, and tact. It also requires a level of candor and humility particularly when you personally have so much at stake (e.g., your unit's reputation and your career).

My experience tells me that much can be accomplished by skippers working together and selflessly when out of earshot of the boss and his staff. This is where the seeds of cooperation and respect are sowed, and the resulting crop to be reaped is a more smoothly running machine when the boss enters the room. There may be some skippers in your group of the "dog-eat-dog" school and they will complicate matters until they can be won over as team players. But the effort is well worthwhile and you will find that you have gained both teammates and friends who will themselves ensure your reputation is enhanced. You should work the problem, not the boss. Your best fellow skippers will help you.

A trivial side benefit of such cooperative conduct is the look on your common boss's face when in a circumstance where he or she expects a problem, you skippers have already solved it. First there will be disappointment that he or she could not have an opportunity to demonstrate leadership or decision making ability. Then there will be a smile of relief and pride that "his" (or her) machine is working smoothly under good leadership. Department heads reading this take note; the same lesson can be applied anywhere in the chain of command.

Studying Your Boss

Of course you will do this throughout your career—not just to be a better officer in the job you now hold, but to give you the background and experience to discharge higher duties if you are called to do so. While serving as a junior officer or department head you were looking *inside* your command when you considered your boss. Now as a skipper you are looking *outside* your command and perhaps on to the Navy as a whole. You now have a larger window on the Navy's world and it is a priceless opportunity. Your boss is now holding a major command or perhaps is a flag officer. You will notice that many of the same skills you have acquired are also required of your boss, but there are now additional skills coming into play.

These skills include integrating the efforts of a large number of units similar to yours and possibly integrating efforts of a number of units with very dissimilar capabilities. They include devising ways to ensure information flows across commands, not just within commands, and that the boss is receiving timely and accurate information he or she needs to make effective decisions. You will also note that your boss is having to lead from a point somewhat removed from where problems are started. Most of these bosses will be keenly aware of command prerogatives (yours) on one hand and the need to maximize the output of the larger organization on the other. If your boss starts to meddle in your command's affairs, it may be that officer lacks confidence in himself or you. The latter should be of particular concern to you. Your first order of business is to conduct matters so that your boss is reassured that you are doing your job—and ever so subtly that you can do it better if your boss focuses on his or her own. Some admirals try to be the captain of the flagship. Flag captains get on by getting out ahead of their admiral. Don't let small things get between you and the boss. Fix them and thank the boss for his or her help in bringing the matter to your attention.

I know one outstanding flag officer who insisted that when he boarded his flagship that he be "bonged" (receive arrival honors) when his foot first hit the quarterdeck. To be bonged earlier, when his car hove into sight, or later when he was being greeted by the officer of the deck and staff watch officer, was unacceptable. Failure to observe this punctilio resulted in much needling of the flag captain who in turn drove his navigator (in charge of watch officers and the quarterdeck) to extreme measures to fix the problem—and fix it they did.

Afterward when asked informally about his insistence on this aspect of rendering honors, the admiral replied, "If they get that right, chances are they will get the rest of it right. The Navy starts with details done well and builds up to major missions done well." But there was an added payoff: the flagship from top to bottom knew the embarked admiral was paying attention and was holding their skipper (and them) to very high and exact standards of performance. A postscript: This flag officer and his battle group successfully completed a very arduous deployment and the former had good reason to sing the praises of his flagship and her skipper.

Command Responsibility and Prerogatives

Often when skippers are convinced they are receiving too many "rudder orders" (detailed instructions from on high and unnecessary for a well-run command) they will lament that the scope of action for today's skippers is much narrower than it used to be. They will cite instant communications and fast information flow among echelons as factors in robbing the commanding officer of time-honored prerogatives. Sometimes such high-level direction is necessary particularly when major political and strategic factors are at issue.

I remember as skipper of an amphibious ship evacuating refugees from Cyprus being told to come up on a high command net and to receive detailed orders directly from the National Military Command Center in Washington. Three command echelons above me were thereby wired out of the problem. It turned out that the nationalities of the refugees (some of whom were badly wounded or injured) were an important factor in selecting a safe haven port in that very troubled region for delivery ashore. But such instances are rare and in almost all cases justified. In my experience complaints about "rudder orders" as inhibiting the exercise of command are overblown—and sometimes involve an attempt by the skipper to be a player and a referee at the same time. As skipper you still have absolute responsibility, accountability, and authority. While modern communications and information systems put the boss at your elbow more than you like, he or she will be very hesitant to overrule you—and thereby accepting personal responsibility for the result in your command.

That is not to say there won't be nervous Nellies and second-guessers in your chain of command (mostly on the staffs), but you are in charge. Nervous staffs imply a nervous admiral somewhere. You need to consider such individuals as "part of the playing field" not an impediment to doing your duty. They will be long on advice and short on accountability.

Several decades ago, one CNO responded to the temptation to put his personal stamp on the way the Navy was run down to the deck-plate level. His fleet-wide messages included directives that many interpreted as telling commanding officers how to perform their duties. While there was a short-term payoff in personalizing leadership from the very top to

A commanding officer on his bridge taking a break from operations to review some paperwork. As executive officer and commanding officer the naval professional has to find the best balance between what must be done and what can be done.
U.S. Naval Institute Photo Archives

the very bottom, a high price was paid in command accountability and engagement in the problems then at hand. More recent CNOs have had a phobia about putting out Navy-wide directives that in any way infringe on the prerogatives of the chain of command—meaning at its most basic level, you as commanding officer.

There is a nugget of wisdom in this discussion that applies to your own reach within your command as skipper. You will be sorely tempted to intervene in one of your departments—a temptation that is particularly acute if you have once been a department head in that field—and bring your expert knowledge to bear. When you experience that temptation ask yourself how you would like your boss to respond in a similar situation and proceed accordingly.

Looking Back

You will find that as you proceed up the career ladder you will often go back to your first experience as a commanding officer, reaching for the wisdom that will serve you well in dealing with the problem now at hand. I have a single piece of advice when you do that: Look at the mistakes you made (and probably weren't noticed at the time) and learn from them as well. Life is more than just leaping from one triumph to another; it also consists of adjusting your fire to reach the target. Among your mementos your first command at sea badge should be the most treasured.

19

On the Waterfront

In the Navy, after you have been in it a certain number of years, everyone knows you, has you labeled, sized up, and catalogued. If you have gotten into trouble, it is lovingly remembered and fixed to your name.

—Capt. A. P. Niblack[1]

You will often hear the phrase, "That is not the way it is on the waterfront," or, "That's not his reputation on the waterfront." The "waterfront" is a shorthand term for the piers where Navy ships are moored when in their home port. It is a term to describe the piers at naval bases such as Mayport, Norfolk, San Diego, Bremerton, Pearl Harbor, Yokosuka, Sasebo, and wherever a number of Navy ships are moored in the same port. And by extension it also describes concentrations of naval air units at naval air stations. These concentrations of warships and aircraft are busy places. There is much work going on. Ceremonies such as changes of command routinely occur. Contractors and naval suppliers conduct their work nearby. Inspections are held. Liberty and leave parties are seen off. Ships and squadrons are welcomed home from and sent on deployment.

The waterfront at your home port is a microcosm of the combat and support forces of the Navy when they are not at sea. When at sea you may steam independently on occasion. On the waterfront you are always in the company of your running mates, squadron mates, similar ship types, and your embarked bosses. Your ship or squadron competes vigorously with its running mates to win the coveted *E* for excellence or to pass some examination with a high score. Your unit's shortcomings are or will be on public view. Your "triumphs" at sea are less visible. The race for professional smartness is joined on the waterfront every day. It is a 24–7 contest. Topside appearance, the turnout of a ship's Sailors, the smartness of the quarterdeck, the prompt and crisp rendering of honors, the way visitors are processed and welcomed, the professionalism of those involved in maintaining pierside security and cleanliness are all closely observed.

Make no mistake, your professional reputation is made at sea. You may shine in Washington or elsewhere ashore, but unless you and your ship or squadron have made your reputation at sea you have not really arrived. When we use the term *waterfront* in the context of an environment or reputation, we are really referring to the real world of being a professional. The waterfront means going to sea or returning from it. A commanding officer's reputation "on the waterfront" is a critical dimension of that officer's service reputation. But you junior readers also have a stake in this race. Just as commanding officers have their reputations on the waterfront, you will learn that many junior officers do also. The wardroom stars start to shine as they make their ship or squadron among the best of the best. Commanding offices will brag about their hard chargers in any gathering with their contemporaries.

For you department heads and executive officers, you have an even bigger stake in this professional environment. Everyone knows which ships or squadrons are smart and which ones are not. The *E*s displayed on the top hamper of the ships at pierside tell their own story. Behind each one is an excellent department head and executive officer. But perhaps your best advertisement is the turnout, demeanor, and attitude of your Sailors. They mix at the head of the pier awaiting transportation, making a phone call, or simply getting a hamburger. In a way most of us do not understand, your ship's reputation and your department get known and the word is passed. This "word" travels both horizontally and vertically up and across the chain of command. There are few secrets about which ships are in trouble and which are not. Never forget that your Sailors and the way they perform are your best advertisement.

For those readers serving afloat at the commodore, carrier air group, or flag levels, you will not be surprised that you also have a reputation that travels both horizontally and vertically. When I was "on the water-front" I remember one flag officer that nearly the entire waterfront hated to go to sea with. It wasn't that he was hard or unfair; it was the fact that bad luck seemed to dog the local operating area whenever his flagship got beyond the sea buoy. Another flag officer made life very exciting for his skippers by calling drills on a moment's notice both at sea and pierside. We brought our ships up to a peak level of readiness and enjoyed playing the game. Still another put more emphasis on pierside smartness than he did on system performance under way. Another flag officer was just the reverse. Each put their distinctive stamp on their forces and that stamp became the basis for their reputation on the waterfront.

Whereas the wardroom or ready room was the cradle of your service reputation as a junior officer, as you progress up the promotion pyramid, the waterfront is one of the major components of the esteem in which you are held.

20

A Naval Dilemma
Blending Tradition and Innovation

> There are two types of fools in this world: those who say
> because it is old it is good and those who say because it is new,
> it is better.
> —Anonymous

The Navy is a conservative service, yet it has been in the forefront of technical innovation. It is conservative because going to sea can be a dangerous profession. The tried and true has saved the lives of many Sailors. The Sailor accepts change but only when it is proved superior to what exists. He does not "bet on the come." She dislikes fads, and change for the sake of change. Although new Sailors like the excitement of change they also admire most old Sailors and strive to be like them. This mixture of reliance on the old, but willingness to accept as much of the new as is proven, is a fact of life that the professional officer understands and accepts.

Most innovators in the Navy have survived difficult voyages. Technical innovators have been more accepted than social innovators. Uriah Levy attempted reforms in the treatment and punishment of Sailors and in the end was successful, but not without some personal cost. Josephus Daniels, a controversial Secretary of the Navy in the early twentieth century, attempted to turn the Navy into a combination boy scout troop, church choir, and temperance meeting. He largely failed and incurred the enmity of sullen seaman and aloof admiral alike. Adm. Elmo Zumwalt attempted to make the Navy more Sailor-friendly in a time of societal upheaval. Some of his reforms stuck and others were discarded amid reverberations that continue down to the present day.

Technical changes are another matter. The Navy accepted armor, the shell-firing gun, and steam propulsion (when the Congress appropriated sufficient funds) and adapted to and improved the submarine and aircraft carrier, after initial development by others. It was and is in the forefront of the development of nuclear propulsion and sea-launched missiles.

But turn the page. The Sailor does not like tinkering with uniforms, shipboard organization and procedures, and most changes dictated by the changing currents of modern society. Racial and gender integration came slowly but came to be accepted as the sine qua non of a truly representative force in the service of the entire nation. These social battles are largely over and fortunately the forces of change won.

What Does This Mean for the Professional Officer?

What does this profile of reaction to change mean to the professional officer? It means being receptive to new ideas, avoidance of practices that have all the earmarks of a fad, and careful consideration before instituting changes in administrative, organizational, and naval societal practices. Some of your Sailors will prod you for changes; others will fight changes tooth and nail. The usual case is that there is merit on both sides. Your job is to build solutions that blend the best of both. It also means that tradition is a powerful tool in the hands of an able leader. Make tradition your ally in the leadership business, not your enemy.

Sailors like to be connected to the naval heroes of the past. A skillful skipper can help make this connection for them. Naval leaders use correct nautical terminology and demonstrate a knowledge of naval history and relate both to the everyday life of today's Sailors. They see today's challenges as an extension of challenges faced by earlier generations of

Sailors. They don't live in the past but are constantly aware of it as the previous generation of naval officers looks over their shoulders to see how the "family business" is prospering. Use tradition as a tool, not a club. Use it as a linkage not a straightjacket. Use it to inspire not as an excuse. Make it relevant to the present, not a crutch set in the past.

The New Emphasis on Picking Innovators as Leaders

There is a trend, some would say that it has been in place for years, toward selecting new flag officers on the basis of their being innovators and not solely because they have done the traditional things well in a lifetime of service. I discern a pattern that suggests that it is *not enough* today to be a proficient and professional operator at sea (though it is the bedrock of our profession), or an astute manager of resources, or an able planner or programmer in the Washington environment. As we pick the new leaders for today's Navy, there is more looking forward, more emphasis on "thinking outside the box" (but not throwing the box away). We want future leaders who see beyond what worked for them and who devise solutions to problems that include reduced resources, different strategic realities, and the need for national power more closely coupled to rapidly changing threats. Old and current career patterns, though still important, are less binding. The professional officer must be sensitive to this changing in the shape of the navigable channel. Be wary of pat answers, going on autopilot, taking "the book" as fixed as the stars, rote responses (e.g., "send a carrier strike group"), current ship and aircraft service life and maintenance metrics, deployment and overhaul rules of thumb.

The Navy's renewed emphasis on resource management, accepting serviceable civilian business practices, adoption of a more flexible fleet response plan, and using lower cost civilian technology when it works in the naval environment are all evidence of a new approach and the need for new top leadership styles.

Make no mistake: the Navy still involves ships, aircraft, and the sea. And we must be expert where they all meet to confront our nation's enemies. But we need to keep our eyes peeled for a better balance between what we need and what has served us so well in the past. Perceptive officers, always aware of the sea state, must be even more alert to its effects on not only the ships under their feet, but also on the national security calculus and on their efforts to shape their own careers.

21

Observing (and Learning from) Admirals at Close Range

So live that thou bearest the strain.
—Capt. Ronald Hopwood[1]

As a junior officer at sea you will rarely see an admiral, particularly in your workplace. You know they have reached the top rungs of the naval profession and many of you are only too aware that you are hanging on to the lower rungs. There seems to be a vast gulf between the two extremes. But your healthy curiosity will cause you to ask, "What makes them different? They were all junior officers once. What have they done (or not) that resulted in such a lofty state?" But if you are really inquisitive these questions will be followed by another: "What can I learn from them?"

In my first sea tour I saw an admiral at close range only once. I was "George" (the junior ensign) in a destroyer at the time. My skipper was told to call on the admiral in his flagship. Both ships were then at sea off the coast of North Korea. For some reason (to teach me something of the naval profession?) the skipper directed that I accompany him. After a wet ride in the destroyer's gig we were ushered into the admiral's in-port cabin. The admiral got right down to business with my skipper while I sat in a corner chair observing the proceedings.

I was impressed by the methodical way the business was conducted, with the admiral's flag secretary placing successive papers before the admiral for discussion and removing those already dealt with. The proceedings were interrupted by the sounds of a crump in the distance and a crash close aboard. The flagship had been taken under shore battery fire and in a moment the flagship returned fire. The admiral seemed to barely notice the interruption but wound up the proceedings after the last agenda item was discussed.

I received a smile and a brief handshake from the admiral. My skipper and I went back to his gig expeditiously and returned to our ship. The duel with North Korean shore batteries lasted most of the afternoon with both U.S. ships firing at the enemy ashore.

I had met Rear Adm. (later Vice Adm.) George W. Dyer, a near legendary figure who had served as one of Adm. "Ernie" King's top aides during World War II and was later a very able and prolific author on naval subjects. What had I learned from this brief encounter? That this admiral was a clear thinker, not concerned about being under fire while conducting a conference with one of his captains, and having complete confidence in his flag captain in engaging the enemy without experiencing the need to rush to the flag bridge to observe and oversee the action. And not least, having the manners and situational awareness to make the acquaintance of perhaps the most junior officer in his command while other matters were uppermost in his mind.

Later as a lieutenant I was aide to an admiral stationed ashore overseas. In that job I had an opportunity to meet and observe at close range a large number of flag officers including two future CNOs. Later as a captain I served as executive assistant to the Chief of Naval Personnel—and it seemed as though every flag officer in the Navy used my office as a waiting room at one time or another. An impressive quality of these successful officers was their warmth of manner toward subordinates and a genuine curiosity as to their interests and concerns.

At this point I will stop the personal memoir and tell you what I distilled from these and other experiences over a full career. In the paragraphs to follow I will offer some seemingly sweeping generalizations to portray the flag officer mystique or way of doing business. Of course, there are exceptions—some of them fairly stark. I readily concede that there is no one-size-fits-all in such descriptions. But I am also convinced that in most descriptors I am not far off the mark in describing the whole. Note the exceptions based on your own observation, but look for the pattern that describes the whole.

Mission Orientation

The average flag officer lets nothing get in the way of his or her unit's mission. To some this will seem like an obsession; to others it will appear as ruthlessness. This focus on the job assigned is a key characteristic of high command. Some have observed that leadership is composed of two components: professional competence and *will*.[2] The will component is mission awareness and determination to see it accomplished. You might ask, "Where do people come in?" People are a factor in this way. Most if not all flag officers know that the mission gets accomplished through people and that they must protect and effectively employ this critical resource—but occasionally a choice must be made and the flag officer focuses on mission. And most Navy men and women know that this must be the case, or we violate a fundamental tenet of our warrior's code.[3] We know that necessary sacrifice is often the edge between winning and losing. Every flag officer of my acquaintance knows that at the end of every command chain there is a Sailor who must be trained, motivated, and led to do his or her job. Moreover the admiral knows that sometimes Sailors must be put in harm's way if an important mission is to be accomplished.

No Cookbook Solutions

Flag officers know that "the book" will only carry one so far. It is no substitute for common sense and mission awareness. Sometimes the rules must be bent. Flag officers are paid to make those decisions and are ready to take full responsibility for them. They tend to be skeptical of "pat"

As naval professionals rise to flag rank they face many challenges that are qualitatively and quantitatively different from those they faced in ship or squadron command. Here a strike group commander welcomes a senior foreign officer in overseeing a major combined operation.
Courtesy of USS Theodore Roosevelt; *photo by PHAN Sheldon Rowley*

answers to difficult questions and those who see problems only in terms of black and white. Most are sensitive to the nuances of *separating* the component parts of a problem and *blending* the elements of a solution.

Candid and Incisive

Most flag officers have an uncanny sense of going straight to the heart of the matter, and pushing aside cant, facades, and underbrush. They are impatient and have no time for the trivial (though they have a good nose for important detail). Most do not "suffer fools gladly" but give good marks to thoughtful and courageous subordinates. They are not looking for "sass" and smart-alecky remarks but they want candor—and a decent respect for their office. Some subordinate officers mistake back talk for guts and "telling it like it is," failing to realize that candor does not require disrespect.

People Are the Key Dimension of Success

Admirals for the most part look behind the rank, position, or surface of a man or woman to see what the inner person is made of. They quickly size up subordinates and seniors and most want a healthy, frank, and candid interchange with them. They recognize that the entire chain of command from top to bottom is composed of flesh and blood, individuals who make mistakes or have at least some inherent weaknesses that must be taken into account. The best flag officers are aware of their own failings as leaders and decision makers and build staffs that compensate for those shortcomings. You can tell a great deal about an admiral by the work climate in his or her staff. Is there a full and frank interchange among staff members, and a readiness to take bad news to the boss after full study of the problem at hand? I vividly remember observing one admiral's chief of staff quietly and unemotionally analyzing a situation facing the command and then step by step leading his boss through the facts and the options on the road to a sound decision. The interchange was characterized by the flag officer's probing, his chief of staff's grasp of the facts, and the atmosphere of candor and mutual respect as they went about the Navy's business.

The best flag officers are also keenly aware that there is a young Sailor or junior officer at the bottom of the chain of command who must carry out his or her decisions. He or she knows that they must set the tone for their commanding officers and not rely on fear of failure and punishment to push for maximum performance.

Fearless Decision Makers

Admirals are paid to make tough decisions, sometimes decisions that will involve life or death, or break careers, or disappoint the boss who had hoped for more, or even call into question their own competence. When we discussed "comers" in an earlier chapter we said that one of their distinguishing characteristics was to be fearless and decisive when faced with difficult problems or decisions. This is not to say they shoot from the hip or are impetuous or slapdash. It means that after they gather the relevant facts (often in an incredibly short amount of time), they act and act firmly, with precision, and with strength. They are rarely second-guessers or waverers. They realize that orders must be firmly given if they are to be carried out promptly and decisively.

Not Captured by Experts

Throughout your career you will depend on experts for advice and for performance of specialized work. A special skill I have observed in most flag officers is the capacity to tap the abilities of those experts but not be captured by them. For most experts the world revolves around their expertise. Their leverage is enhanced by the fact that there is often no substitute for their expertise. Successful leaders know how to tap that expertise but not be unduly constrained by the point of view that an expert brings to the task at hand. Experts like to point out that something "can't be done" or if it is done it may have disastrous consequences. But the mark of an able flag officer (or skipper) is the ability to know when the expert gets beyond his or her field.

I have watched excellent flag officers sit with a group of experts, sifting their advice, asking questions that push the limits of the experts' knowledge, probing for the key element in the problem at hand, and then integrating information across the board to come up with a workable solution the experts did not identify but nonetheless is suitable to the circumstances. The flag officers undertook this exercise with tact, knowledge of their own limitations, a willingness to learn, and a healthy curiosity. You will have no more broadening experience than watching such problem-solving maestros at work. You don't run roughshod over experts; you tap their knowledge and use it to solve your problem, not necessarily theirs.

Intense Loyalty to Their Bosses

By loyalty I mean that flag officers make it their business to know in detail their boss's objectives and give full effort to seeing that they are met. They almost invariably put themselves in their boss's shoes before they make a decision and factor how their decision works into the boss's plan or policy. Most times they will do this even in circumstances where perceptive staff officers know their own admiral would prefer to act otherwise.

As an aside I may say that sometimes this loyalty is carried too far and overlooks the larger good in pursuit of the objectives assigned. But this is a highly judgmental matter. If we look at Nelson's example we see evidence both of loyalty (to John Jervis, Lord St. Vincent, and his plans and policies related to Nelson's pursuit of the French fleet that led to Trafalgar), and something less in the "blind eye" that Nelson turned to Hyde-Parker at Copenhagen. A more modern example, something not fully examined in the naval literature, is the official and personal relationship between Admiral Nimitz and Admiral King in World War II. Nimitz was loyal to King but did not hesitate to take a different course when the circumstances dictated. He took any later chastisement from King stolidly without any rancor as far as we know. King was a tough man to work for, but Nimitz had the quiet inner courage to stand up to him without seeking unnecessary confrontation.

They Are Not Caretakers; They Expand the Envelope

You will run across many officers (including some flag officers) who perform more like caretakers than pushers and movers. Their objective is to leave things much the way they found them or perhaps with a little effort making improvements at the margin. They play the hands they are dealt rather than getting a new deal, or playing the full envelope provided by the rules, or even playing a new game—all with the objective of really improving unit performance. As a junior officer, perhaps a division officer or department head, you will not have a great deal of latitude—but there is some there. Find it and exploit it for your division, for your department, for your Sailors, and for your unit.

As you become more senior you will find the constraints that limit your actions are somewhat more elastic and you have more room to maneuver. Flag officers have a great deal of latitude on how they construe their tasking and their missions. Alas, some remain in the groove set by their predecessors and do not really make a difference. Most flag officers insist on making a difference and will push their juniors hard to expand the envelope of what can be done and then go ahead and do it.

Admiration of Good Operators

Most flag officers admire good operators, perhaps because most of them were also good operators when commanders and captains. I mean ship handlers, aviators, tacticians, strike group maestros, and so on. I have seen admirals seek out the best operators and vicariously relive some key moment in their own careers. But sometimes this focus on operations clouds their view on the best people needed for a particular job. Some good operators are so-so planners, staff officers, or managers. This bias sometimes extends to selection boards. I have heard two chiefs of Naval Personnel decry some selection board results with remarks along these lines: "All they have given me to fill important assignments are good ship drivers and throttle jockeys, when what I most need at this moment are good communicators, comptrollers, information processors, and weapons acquisition professionals [etc.]." While this bias for operators is understandable it has become less pronounced in recent years as the importance and leverage of key shore and joint positions have become more apparent.

Details and Delegation Are Both Important

Admirals must delegate. They can't be flagship skipper and admiral at the same time without risking that both jobs will be done poorly. Most do delegate well and ensure that in so doing they are properly informed of what they *must* know. This takes work and self-control and the temptation is almost irresistible when the stakes are large and there is great pressure from on high. No admiral can afford to operate on the policy that "when any mistake is made, I want to make it." This is a recipe for micromanaging and the risk is that the admiral won't have enough information to micromanage. In my experience there are very few flag officers that don't follow this advice. That is not to say they don't worry or fret, but they recognize the danger of interference.

Admiral Nimitz during World War II represents the acme of following such advice. He had a phobia against trying to take decision-making authority away from tactical commanders—even when the stakes were very high indeed. He constantly cautioned his staff and Washington staffs against interference with the commander on the scene. In all this there is a good nautical analogue in the rules of the road. The privileged vessel must maintain course and speed until *extremis*. The good admirals (and most are) have a keen nose for *extremis*.

But able flag officers also understand that a nose for the important detail is vital to good decision making. Their questions to the staff and skippers are usually rooted in looking for that important detail or for the answer that conveys the quality of the whole. In my experience most flag officers have a seeming uncanny ability to tease out what is important from what is not, to ask just the right (and often unsettling) question. As a staff officer your greatest learning experience is to foresee such questions and prepare the answers. But beyond that is the need to prepare yourself to be asking similar questions at some future date.

Leadership Is More Than Giving Orders

The naïve think that orders are the beginning and end to being an effective leader or manager. Admirals know better. They know they must install and maintain systems that ensure that their will is carried out, and that if matters go awry there are feedback channels to inform them. The work is in the doing and seeing that it is done. You junior officers take heed: your Sailors will quickly see through any exhortation not backed up by effective follow-through. They hate speeches but respect decisive action.

Keeping the Boss Informed

Every flag officer that I have known felt an acute responsibility for keeping the boss informed. I sat in a four-star combatant commander's office once and watched the boss pick up the hot line to tell the CNO of some breaking development that was of keen public interest. The commander knew instinctively that he had to get the news to the boss as soon as possible. On other occasions I have been present when matters came up in a conference and the senior admiral present, sensing a major problem or opportunity, insisted on the necessity of letting his boss know *now* what was going on.

Some of this alertness goes back to the loyalty descriptor discussed earlier in this chapter. But I believe it is also based on a keen understanding that the information channels are critical to decision making at all levels. Moreover, they know and expect they too will be kept informed of important developments by their subordinates. This sensitivity is a key attribute of flag officers. They may sleep on a decision but not on delaying information flow.

Staying in Control of Events

Some use the unflattering term, "control freaks." The core of leadership is command and control and the communications and intelligence to make them work. You are correct in assuming that admirals are interested in and insist on control. That is their business and you forget it at your professional peril. The most difficult challenges that a naval officer faces as he proceeds from command upward into the flag ranks are to establish control mechanisms for each organization that he or she heads, mechanisms that enable them to effectively wield their authority (command). Admirals know that almost instinctively. Their most pressing questions and concerns will center on the formulation and transmittal of their instructions and orders and how they can adjust or modulate their control to fit circumstances as they arise.

A few flag officers rely on the mechanisms that worked for them as skippers of ships or squadrons. They soon find that they are in a different league as flag officers and what they took for granted as a three- or four-striper no longer works at the flag level. The beginning of a staff officer or skipper's wisdom is to understand that the admiral in charge has a whole new set of requirements for information and advice if he or she is to do the job. The stubborn skipper or staff officer fights this tendency but the nimble and prescient officer works to fill the need.

What Does All This Mean to Your Own Performance?

You might respond, "Thanks for the tour of the horizon on what admirals worry about, but what does it mean for me?" Most will see instinctively that much of what works for admirals will work for you or can be adapted to do so. If you are an ambitious and professional officer, you are looking around the next bend to see what is expected of you as you take on higher responsibilities. Moreover, as you become more senior you will find that you deal more and more with admirals. It helps to understand what is on their minds—because some of it will be foreign to your experience. Look on this chapter as a familiarization course on the care and feeding of flag officers. You can learn it now or you can learn it later, but learn it you will if you stay in the Navy long enough.

22

Combat
Will You Measure Up?

> There is nothing quite so uplifting as to be shot at—
> without effect.
> —Winston Churchill, reflecting on his active service as a junior officer

It may surprise you to learn that there have been and are many old Sailors and admirals in the Navy who have never been in combat. They may have directed or supported combat operations. They may have sailed in troubled waters. They may have launched ordnance at an enemy many miles away. However, it is a fact that many have never heard the explosion of enemy ordnance near them. They may have awards or decorations for their work but few have them for valor in combat. Part of this is an artifact of the Cold War where many operations involved high readiness and arduous deployments but few shots fired in anger (at them). Of course, the Korean War and Vietnam War are exceptions but even there, a flagship or naval headquarters was seldom under fire and most Navy men or women never heard or saw an "incoming." Though our Navy's submariners undertook many courageous feats in intelligence gathering during the Cold War, very few were shot at in the doing. The risks accepted were high—including passage of minefields—but in large part due to their professionalism few were taken directly under fire.

The simple fact of the matter is that in the modern era (say the last thirty to forty years or so) few Navy men and women can be said to be *combat* veterans—if we define combat as the *exchange* of weapons fire. Most have supported, directed, or been near combat operations but few have been in the crosshairs of the enemy. The obvious exceptions are those Navy airmen who have flown combat missions, delivered ordnance, and received fire; SEALs; and those surface and riverine warriors who have received hostile fire. The point of this quick assessment is that you too may go through a naval career training for combat but never really experience it. You may respond, "What a lousy way to spend my life; working hard and never getting to do what I was trained to do!" What you have missed in this assessment is that your mission was and is to train and work hard to limit the necessity of combat. Welcome to the world of deterrence and modern warfare that puts a premium on striking from a distance and denying the enemy a clean shot. Early in my career I had the frightening experience of having a shipmate shot down beside me while he was firing his weapon at the enemy. I view most modern naval operations and warfare as a distinct improvement over the old days.

You may agree, but add, "What if I am placed under fire in a future conflict? How do I know I will meet the test?" The simple answer is that you don't know but the odds are very high that you will meet that challenge successfully. You will find that your training, the world's best in our profession, and the leadership demonstrated by you and your chain of command will see you through. While you may not enjoy the experience, you will be proud of your service and have a special bond with those who served with you. After all very, very few of the Sailors present at Pearl Harbor on December 7, 1941 had ever before been shot at or delivered fire on an enemy. I know of no cases where they fell short of the mark.

How Do You Prepare Yourself for Combat?

The easy answer is that you train very hard and test yourself at every opportunity. Capt. Slade Cutter, one of the Navy's greatest combat leaders, put his experience in World War II this way:

Everyone was eager to do his part. We knew why we were doing it—for our mothers, fathers, wives, and sweethearts back home. We were a close-knit-group, and every man aboard depended on his shipmates, whether they were an officer or enlisted. We didn't feel like we were heroes. We just had a job to do, and we did it the best we could, *the way we were trained.* It was never a one man show, either. *Everybody had an important job to do, and there was very little margin for error.*

We sought harm's way you know, and my crewmen wanted to do that. But they also wanted to be brought back. I brought them back.[1]

While the immediacy and danger of combat cannot be duplicated in training, there are some surrogate experiences that prepare you for it. Some of these experiences start in childhood and continue into your undergraduate work in college or at the academy. I have in mind athletics, particularly competitive athletics where you are pitted against an able opponent. If there is physical contact, so much the better. It is there that you learn the pain of losing and the joy of winning, of playing through aches and pains, of reaching down and drawing up that last ounce of courage and stamina needed to prevail or to acquit yourself honorably. Such experiences may well be at the intramural and not the varsity level, but the principles involved are the same. The advantage of organized athletics (e.g., college varsity sports) is that you see the advantages of training and conditioning. A pickup game of touch football or rugby relies more on athleticism (not all are so blessed) to carry one thorough. However, in organized athletics, there is a "commanding officer" whose job it is to see that you are prepared to perform. That individual is called "coach."

But even the noncontact or individual sports bring some of the feel of combat. There is an opponent whose objective it is to beat you and you must rely on yourself, your athletic prowess, and your wits to win. In athletics we are not looking for physical punishment—either to deal it out or receive it—but on establishing the will and stamina to prevail—where the stakes are real and immediate.

Capt. Slade Cutter was awarded the Navy Cross for his decisive leadership during World War II. Cutter was the consummate naval professional who trained the way he fought. He believed a naval career was all about connecting the dots between the naval officer and winning. *Courtesy of Anne Cutter McCarthy*

There is another dimension to athletics that bears mentioning: getting and staying in good physical condition. Veterans of combat will tell you that one of the most important ingredients of success is stamina. The last fighter standing wins. Most combat veterans will cite the fatigue that constant combat or the prospect of such imposed on them physically and mentally. You need to pay attention to your physical condition not only because you need it to finish the race to professional success, but also because it is perhaps your most important advantage when the bullets start to fly.[2] You should look on your physical condition as your fuel tank and keep it topped off for use when needed and to stretch those miles for the long haul. You are filling your tank when you pay attention to your physical fitness regimen and diet, perfect the ability to catnap (only during lulls!), and keep your sense of humor in times of stress.

Even more important than athletics and physical fitness is the role of realistic and constant training. In my discussions with Captain Cutter, it became clear that athletics had a role in nurturing his warrior spirit and in his conditioning. He was at sea in a combat area when the war started *and* when it ended. But when one reads his biography as a whole it becomes apparent that the training he received (and those who provided it) were superb and he benefited mightily from that peacetime effort. While some training doctrine gets thrown out the window as irrelevant when the first bullet is fired, most of it is retained and valued for the mind-set it fosters.

In today's world of sophisticated simulators and live fire exercises (the former were nonexistent and the latter very limited when Captain Cutter was a junior officer) training is better than it has ever been. Some treat the simulators as computer games but when you are fully engaged in a simulation, you are as close to realism (absent the pucker factor) as you are likely to get.

When we say that training is the Navy's primary peacetime mission, we are saying that war fighting and survival are the payoffs. Those who despise training and look forward to the real thing are not really pros; they are rank amateurs and will soon be found out. A pro trains to win—whether in the ring, on the athletic field, in a cockpit simulator, or in a weapons delivery exercise. An amateur goes into combat to "feel the experience" with an empty head and an empty fuel tank.

There is yet another dimension to preparation for combat: mental preparation. Try to visualize future combat and the role of your weapons system. Are you simply a risk taker who is betting the odds, or are you a calculating killer who is determined to win? Have you rehearsed the decisions you will likely be required to make? Have you fully internalized the pressures you will face? Training and physical fitness will only carry you so far: your attitude and your reasoning are more likely to be the X factor that provides the edge.

Have you gone through the scenarios from beginning to end and asked "what if" questions and then gone on to study to find out their answers? The winners in battle are professionalism, the capacity to decide what to do, and the will to win. This is where unit esprit comes in. Combat psychologists have long known that we fight for our shipmates ("buddies") more than such abstract symbols as the flag, home, and hearth. We refuse to let them down, we sacrifice ourselves for their survival in the sure knowledge they will do the same for us, we demand more of ourselves because others depend on us. If your unit is "tight" and a band of brothers (and sisters), there is a direct payoff in battle. Too much goes into unit esprit to discuss it here. But you know it when you see it: respected skippers, a clear and shared sense of mission, a pride in professionalism, and a real consideration for shipmates. If your unit has a high esprit de corps, I can guarantee that it and you will perform well in battle.

The Danger of the Peacetime Mind-Set

Terence Robertson, the biographer of Capt. Frederic John Walker, RN, has observed: "The Navy in peacetime and the Navy at war are vastly different affairs. Officers who had been social lions and earmarked for high rank in 1939 had been known to fail on the battlefield; others who had spurned the niceties of peacetime service and suffered for it were proving indomitable and sometimes brilliant leaders in war."[3]

One may argue that such a portrait is overdrawn, but the U.S. Navy went through a similar experience and trauma during the months following the Japanese attack on Pearl Harbor on December 7, 1941. Some officers—even comers—who had successfully navigated the peacetime career path fell short of the mark when the bullets started to fly. It was not that they did not have personal courage. It was that they were in many cases overly cautious and not "battle-minded." The greatest Navy defeat after Pearl Harbor was at Savo island where the loss of four cruisers was attributed by Admiral Nimitz to a lack of battle-mindedness.

In the peacetime Navy of the 1920s and 1930s and into the early 1940s a great premium was placed on doing things by the book, not sticking one's neck out, putting a major effort into achieving good scores on unrealistic peacetime gunnery drills. Commanding officers of major ships were well into middle age. Even the submarine force, with a reputation as a youthful service, had skippers who were in some cases seven or eight years senior to their executive officers. Some of the shortcomings of the officer corps were due to a promotion system wherein officers stagnated at the junior grades and then ran rapidly through the senior grades to retirement. But most of the problem flowed from a peacetime focus on economy of operation, formal exercises increasingly divorced from the realities of contemporary combat, and a service atmosphere where risk takers and innovators went unrewarded.

The net result of these shortcomings was that some of the Navy's senior officers were found wanting when they went into combat. Most were transferred to training and administrative billets ashore and served well while a crop of battle-minded more junior officers were advanced to fill the gaps.

What are the lessons for today's officers in this experience? First, don't throw the baby out with the bathwater. It is not that the emphasis on economy, regulations, and peacetime smartness are unimportant. They are needed most of the time. But it is too easy a leap from observing the stumbles of brilliant peacetime leaders in wartime to the conclusion that the promotion and screening systems are to blame. The same peacetime system that produces some wartime duds also produces the brilliant leaders who win in battle. The point is that the pressures of combat often expose previously undetected, and perhaps even undetectable, weaknesses. The real lesson is that there is an entirely new overlay of requirements imposed by combat and wartime conditions. We do our best to train and structure our forces in peacetime to meet war requirements but often we don't get it exactly right. Never forget when you are bogged down in the details of preparing for an important exam (which puts a very high premium of going by the book), operational readiness exercises (which usually involve elaborate safety precautions), or administrative inspections (which focus on paperwork rather than morale and readiness) that the real world of combat lies just over the horizon.

What is the reverse of that coin? Some officers are mediocre peacetime officers and lions in combat. When peace returns they receive respect for their wartime exploits but in many cases they are not best suited for operating the peacetime Navy and building the Navy of the future. This is not a black and white exercise. Many do both well—and others do both poorly. But we should not be surprised that a good many do one much better than the other. Your objective should be what it has always been: to do all tasks well, but keeping the duties of today in a longer perspective. Recognize the peacetime mind-set is only a tool to get the peacetime job done. When war is in the offing you must go back to your toolbox for skills that fit the task at hand.

In closing let me add a few words about the word *courage*. Don't mistake bravado, recklessness, or dashing about as courage. In their search for the dramatic the cinema, television, and some books often set a misleading example. Much courage is of the quiet kind: calmly sizing up the enemy and then deftly delivering the critical blow. John Buchan once remarked: "It was a wise man who said that the biggest kind of courage was being able to sit still."[4]

23

The Intangibles of the Naval Profession

> Every commander should keep constantly before him
> the great truth, that to be well obeyed, he must be
> perfectly esteemed.
> —John Paul Jones[1]

You have heard the words many times before: honor, courage, commitment. They are difficult to measure, to teach, and to make relevant to the everyday tasks of life. But they have one thing in common: they require a willingness "to pay the price." In today's society if you are to pay the price, you want to know what you are getting for it. What distinguishes military service from civilian occupations (and even from some of the other professions) is that the military professional doesn't ask the price—or the reward, if any. Honor, courage, and commitment are parts of what they are, not negotiable as part of a transaction.

I have known naval officers who operated a quart low on honor, courage, and commitment. Some of them became successful in achieving the tangible rewards conferred on an able serving officer. But I know of no case where they were not found out. In many cases the discovery happened late in their careers and their prospects turned south as their true reputations became known. The first to see through deception or a facade were the individual's contemporaries. Close behind were their shipmates. Alas, sometimes lagging the pack were the individuals' bosses.

There is a lesson in the late discovery of those who fail to meet the test of honor, courage, and commitment. When you assess an individual as a shipmate or senior, are you looking behind the surface accomplishment to see whether the individual is paying the price, climbing on the shoulders of others, or using deceit to achieve show? Do his or her shipmates and contemporaries respect the individual?

Being a Good Shipmate

This is one of the most treasured accolades that can be conferred by those who serve with you. Because so much of today's Navy is based ashore, the term *shipmate* has taken on a larger scope and is frequently applied to any person who has served with you at sea or ashore. What is a good shipmate? First of all he or she is someone you trust—even with your life or honor. Second, a good shipmate is one who does the right thing instinctively. The "right thing" is more often in the moral than the physical realm. It is the quiet demonstration of courage in personal matters and in doing one's duty. Good shipmates are there when you need them. They commit themselves to their unit, their shipmates, and themselves in that order. Their loyalty is commonplace, not something that is purchased.

You may ask, "What does being a good shipmate have to do with professional performance?" The simple answer is that it is almost impossible to perform well without the support of others. As you become more senior, you will gradually realize that you have depended on others more than they have depended on you. You can only be effective in a naval setting by working through and with others. That does not mean that you "use" them (though a few do); it means that they are a part of your and your unit's sinews in achieving the mission. At a more basic level they are necessary for your survival, as you are necessary for theirs. These bonds are founded on honor, courage, and commitment—not on self-interest, opportunism, and exploitation. Simply put, honor, courage, and commitment are the basic foundations of your profession, your performance, and if it comes your way, success in being a professional officer. If you don't have them or don't take them on board during your cruise through Navy life, you probably will fail and find yourself isolated when you most need support. You have not turned into a professional but into a careerist who, to use the aviator's term, "must constantly watch his (or her) six" and be afraid of exposure. This watchfulness and the suspicion that it engenders are the enemies of unit esprit and self-respect.

These simple facts are often overlooked or taken for granted by midshipmen or junior officers who may see them as the dry and intangible subject matter of a leadership course, bumper stickers with little operational meaning, or hectoring by old windbags enjoying their retirement but divorced from the "real Navy." You accept such a judgment at your professional peril.

Honor, courage, and commitment are not things you distill out of an amalgam of professional qualities. You instinctively know them when you see them. One of my close friends was a legend on the athletic fields at the Naval Academy and one of the top combat skippers of World War II. Until the day he died he maintained an aura of professional competence and selflessness. When you were in his presence you could feel the real strength of the man—his honesty and candor, his will to never spare himself, his willingness to accept his responsibilities in the face of poor health, his rejection of excuses, his embrace of the warrior ethic: "Never complain, never explain." After knowing him for some time, I told myself, "This is the man I would want to go into combat with. He is straight and true and a man or woman would be proud to call him 'shipmate.'" Will your future shipmates say that of you when you are measured against the professional yardstick of the Navy calling?

24

Assessing Career Advice

We may give you advice, but we cannot inspire conduct.
—François duc de La Rochefoucauld, *Maxims*

Career advice is a cottage industry both within and outside the Navy. Any number can play and do. Naval career advice is often offered and indeed you may often seek it. This book is evidence in support of both points. One thing is certain: you will receive a great deal of it. Indeed, at least once a year you are required to receive counseling on your performance incident to the preparation of your fitness reports. It is but a short step from performance counseling to career counseling—as this book and its predecessor demonstrate.

Navy career advice is based on three factors: (1) the obvious signposts of career advancement—but bear in mind that the obvious is often overlooked, (2) the naval profession is "closed" (entry from the bottom and selection for advancement from within), and (3) as a junior officer you are a captive audience. Senior naval officers take a keen interest in the professional development of their subordinates and advice is often the result. You will have a tough job in separating the wheat from the chaff, the general from the unique, the important from the trivial, and the relevant from the "beside the point." This chapter is intended to help you sift through the advice received. Here are some tests.

Has the Adviser an Axe to Grind?

Some advisers are so narrowly focused on their own warfare community or their own experiences (good or bad) that they attempt to justify their own career choices or explain their own career disappointments by using you as a captive audience. These officers usually see the advantages and pitfalls of their own career path without fully recognizing your preferences and capabilities.

Does the Adviser Have the Relevant Knowledge and Experience to Offer Advice?

Does the adviser have up-to-date knowledge on the career paths in your community and know how the assignment, screening, and promotion processes work? Or, are they relatives with little familiarity with service practices and norms (Uncle Ben was a lieutenant colonel in the Air Force twenty-five years ago)? How wide is the gap between what your chain of command is telling you and the adviser's suggestions?

Has the Adviser Been Successful in His or Her Own Career to This Point?

Beware the sour adviser who has encountered a disappointment in his or her own career and blames the system. Their advice may be more intended to soothe their own egos than to be of assistance to you. At a more basic level, do you look for advice from successful practitioners or from those who have hit a bump in the road? However, do not dismiss advice too quickly from those who have encountered a career disappointment. Each such story contains an object lesson—perhaps not the one the adviser intends. As you become more senior you will encounter some career wrecks in progress and you can learn from them almost as much as from the success of others.

Is the Adviser Really Interested in You and Your Career?

Some would-be advisers have no vested interest in giving you good advice. In many cases they don't know you very well and do not have a good understanding of your strengths and weaknesses. In the absence of such knowledge, how could they give you good advice? The best advice usually comes from those with both the requisite knowledge and a keen interest in you and your career development. The worst advice comes from the gullible, the glib, those who are impressed by superficialities, and those who see you as an audience not a partner in your professional development. I have found that you rarely get informed advice from your contemporaries even though they may be friends and have your best interest at heart. That said, you can never get too many data points to form your own opinion.

Does the Advice Reflect a Fad?

The Navy goes through fads just as any other institution does. The saving factor in the Navy setting is that the service is a conservative one that has to be convinced of the need for change. After World War II naval aviation and the submarine service drew the attention of most officer aspirants. In the last two decades in particular surface warfare has made a dramatic comeback in popularity, in part because of the increased professionalism in that warfare specialty. Many officers were attracted to the engineering duty and aeronautical engineering duty specialties after World War II because of the advanced education involved and the lure of a future spent mostly ashore and not deployed. While not all fads, these attractions wax and wane.

There was a time when some of the best naval aviators were attracted to test pilot training or assignment to the Blue Angels. Some still are. In later years assignment to Top Gun became attractive. Fleet replacement squadrons have been popular since their establishment in the late 1950s.

One sanity check on advice is to attempt to assess it as a passing fancy or a permanent change. If you get advice to seek an "in" subspecialty, it may be too late.

How Might I Rank Order Advisers and Advice?

The key to good advice is seeking the most informed sources, sources that are current and have a broad view of the profession. I caution that seniority is not always an indication the adviser is current in the field in which they are offering advice. What seniority probably does indicate is that they have been successful in what *they* did. But even the best informed professionally may not have sufficient knowledge about you to offer good advice.

I have received and given a great deal of career advice over the years and have seen firsthand how the assignment, screening, and promotions systems work. In the paragraphs to follow there is a rough rank ordering of my biases on the quality of the sources of advice. Don't take this rank ordering too literally. Some sources in the middle of the list may deserve to be nearer the top in some circumstances.

1. *Your commanding officer.* Your skipper almost by definition has stood in your shoes. Moreover, he or she is probably in your warfare specialty and knows what it takes to succeed (he or she is, after all, your skipper and was carefully screened for the job). Moreover, your skipper knows you and your strengths and weaknesses. That officer is motivated to give you good advice. The only downside may be gaps in their specific knowledge of the assignment system and where you stand vis-à-vis your professional competitors. Bottom line: Your skipper's advice deserves your close attention and respect.

2. *Other successful officers in your specialty.* Right after your skipper are other senior officers who have demonstrated their performance

and some considerable knowledge of how things work in the Navy's world of assignments and promotions. Sometimes these officers are also your mentors and have some knowledge about your qualifications.

3. *Detailers.* Detailers have a unique position in your set of career advisers. They have knowledge both of you and how the system works. However in addition they have perhaps the best understanding (outside of a selection board) of how you stack up with your running mates. The detailer has in all likelihood conversed with you by phone or e-mail. That officer has your preference card, can see your summary performance score, and knows what screening and promotion boards are looking for. However, detailers have two blind spots: First, most do not have the historical perspective on the tides of change. They focus on today's balance among billets, bodies, preferences, and optimal career patterns. Second, they face the workplace pressures of having to fill billets and keep everyone as happy as possible. Although horror stories will always occur, my experience is that detailers are candid, informed, and have their fingers on the pulse of their warfare community. When your detailer gives you advice, listen and leave your biases behind.

4. *Mentors.* The mentor is most likely your current or former commanding officer or another senior officer who has expressed an interest in you, an interest perhaps as deep as friendship. Almost by definition mentors know you; the only question is how up to speed are they on current assignment, screening, and promotion practices. In my experience mentors provide additional data points in the spectrum of receiving advice; listen up but better yet listen to your detailer and your skipper.

5. *Officers who have experienced career disappointments.* It pays to be skeptical when listening to members of this group, but listen closely anyway. Try to identify their biases (e.g., luck, politics, system quirks) and look for the nuggets such as paths best not

taken, performance traits that work against success, and the role of taking responsibility for your own missteps.

6. *Messmates and contemporaries.* You will be subjected to a great deal of advice from members of this group. Unfortunately, most of it is uninformed (though perhaps well-intentioned). Many have very little understanding of how the world of assignments and promotions works. They have not been your detailer, your boss, or mentor. They may think they know you but consciously or subconsciously they are superimposing your situation on their own and the match is likely imperfect.

In looking over this list of potential career advisers, you are probably catching a glimmer of a multisided matrix with axes portraying the degree of the adviser's system knowledge, knowledge about you, knowledge about the competition, and the breadth of their perspective. We won't belabor the point in this chapter except to say that an assessment of advice is multidimensional and requires good self-knowledge and information on the career environment.

A good question might be: Where does the book before the reader fall in this spectrum of advice and advisers? The strength of the book lies in its system knowledge and breadth of perspective. Its weaknesses are that it cannot know you the reader personally and that by taking a broader perspective some of the details pertaining to the current situation may be changing or otherwise not up to date. On the other hand, the book is the product of many years of conversations with midshipmen and officers across the seniority spectrum. Thus I may not know you personally but the odds are high I know somebody who is very much like you. The book is intended as an aid to decision making rather than as a substitute for the advisers you will encounter in the course of a full career. If you want up-to-the-minute detail on the current system, you are advised to talk to your detailer or visit the Naval Personnel Command home page.

A former Commandant of Midshipmen at the Naval Academy warned midshipmen to take all career advice with a grain of salt. That is still good advice—but it presumes you have made the effort to stay well informed so that you may be skeptical and receptive in equal measure.

25

Perspectives of a Naval Career

The most successful career must show a waste of strength that
might have moved mountains.
—E. M. Forster[1]

A Macro View

Stand back for a moment and look at a full career as it applies to many
naval officers. Assume that such a career is twenty-six to thirty years in
length with the officer rising to the rank of captain. The first half of the
career centers on learning the profession and filling the many billets
involved in operating and maintaining naval forces. While ashore most
will be involved in supporting current forces and developing future
forces. The second half of the career centers on commanding current
forces while at sea and managing the Navy's current resources and
developing future forces while serving ashore.

To develop professionally an officer must perform well in the first
half of his or her career to get a shot at the second half. He or she must
perform well in the second half to get a spot in the Navy's top leadership
(flag rank). The dividing line between the first half of your career and
the second half is your command tour in the rank of commander. When
you say, "I relieve you, sir," you have passed several milestones—all
important. You have taken command for the first time. You have started
the transition to becoming a member of the Navy's top talent pool.
While relying on what you have learned to date, you have started on the
voyage of acquiring the new skills needed ashore and afloat to lead and

manage the vast enterprise called the U.S. Navy. Your career will never be the same after you pass this transition point.

For junior officers who have gotten this far, that first command (usually in the rank of commander) is the compass you steer by. Everything you have done to that point has been to prepare yourself for that moment. If you don't get that command tour, because others performed better or because the numbers involved mean few can be chosen, you still have important tasks to perform. But they will not be in leading today's Navy and performing in the top roles in building the Navy of the future.

The touchstone of this progression is superb comparative performance. It starts very early in your career and builds momentum as you progress from billet to billet. If at every step of your career you are the best performer in your command—in your rank, skill set, and promise of future growth—you are well on your way to flag rank. If you are nearly the best you have a shot at professionally rewarding command tours in the second half of your career and your hat is in the ring for flag rank. If your performance as recorded by successive commanding officers puts you "in the pack" at every step, the second half of your career will be much like the first. You will have important jobs, but you will not be tapped to lead today's Navy or have a central role in preparing for its future.

Some readers may observe: "What if I find myself (perhaps through no fault of my own) on a poor career track? I may be in what you have called an 'orphan community.' I may be the best at what I do, but if what I do is not important to the Navy's leadership at screening and promotion time, what hope is there for me for a full and successful career?" Excellent questions and the answers are found at several levels. First and most obvious is to do all you can—even very early in your career—to avoid orphan communities or dead ends, or communities that historically have not been well treated by screening and promotion boards. Sometimes officers end up in such communities by their own passing fancy, or by becoming fascinated by the professional content of that community—and future promotions be damned—or by going with the flow, or by viewing their naval career as a short-term proposition—only to find later that they want to stay for a full career. This comes back to knowing yourself and to exerting yourself early in your career—even during your days as a midshipman or officer candidate.

The second level of response is to observe that if you do your best—even in a community with a poor track record of promotions—you will come to the attention of the people who count—your bosses, your detailer, and future selection and screening boards. You may face steeper odds than those in the more favored communities, but you can still be a player. You will also find that the superb job you do ashore—where community associations often do not matter as much—will push you toward the front of the class come promotion time. I know one officer in an orphan community who turned outstanding performance in that community into four stars. I know another officer who served his entire career in two so-called orphaned communities and ended up with three stars and as commander of a numbered fleet. The number of similar cases is beyond an easy count. Don't give up; perform!

There is another factor in play when we discuss your performance and the comparative odds of promotion by warfare community. You may be in a front-line warfare community but you seek the "fur-lined" billet, the most congenial duty station, regular working hours, the job where you can start feathering your nest for eventual retirement. If you succeed in these pursuits, you have scant basis for complaining later that you were overlooked at screening or promotion time. Detailers run into this situation all the time: An officer doesn't want to pay the "full price" of tough assignments but wants to stay in the mainstream of the profession and be a competitor for screening and promotion. Ladies and gentlemen, it doesn't work that way!

A Micro View

What are the components of your professional performance? There are four: you, your performance as a pro, the mission at hand, and your commanding officer. You must study each to prosper. The first has to do with knowing yourself and your strengths and weaknesses—reinforcing the former and remedying the latter. Knowing your job is the same as professional competence—in your division, in your department, on the bridge, at your battle station, or in the cockpit. Knowing your mission becomes your first glimpse of the big picture after training. Knowing your commanding officer means learning from that officer—for good or for ill. The skipper is the team captain. Your job is to do more than just please the skipper; you must crawl inside his or her skin and see your job from his or her perspective. Are you a burden or a key structural member?

With knowledge of these basics in hand—self, being a pro, mission, and your skipper—you must launch yourself into each working day with gusto, determination, curiosity, careful concern for your shipmates, and a healthy sense of humor. Don't run from hard work. Take Admiral King's motto to heart: "Difficulties are things that it is our business to solve."

A Mind-Set

You should enter into each job with a mind-set that says: This is the most important job for me in the entire world. But go further: The way I do this job will make a difference. Too many officers enter into their duties either looking behind them at their last job (particularly if it involved going to sea) or forward to their next job. They are not tending to business—doing today's work today. Others are not convinced that their present job is important and that it doesn't really matter how well they do it. Both attitudes—not focusing on the present job and not believing it is important—are death blows to any naval career, and perhaps any other. Sure, look ahead to your future career and back to your successes and mistakes—but stay focused on the job at hand. It really is the most important job in your career to date. If you have and keep that attitude, you will prosper and the Navy will get a handsome return on its investment in you.

A Set of Bumper Stickers

At this point in our journey through your career in prospect and retrospect you don't need another set of bumper stickers and a list of dos and don'ts. Settle for five simple words to define a successful naval career: *mission, people, performance, command,* and *sea.* If all you take away from this book and its predecessor are these five words you will have the outline for a successful career and have the preparation needed to leave a legacy of service. In fact these five words could be the core structure of a speech on what the Navy is all about. This book covers the essential territory and adds structure to the key word outline. Beyond those words are additional books on the mechanics of the naval profession. And beyond that is your experience, gained block by block, as you become a naval professional.

You will receive a great deal of advice in your career, some of it good. The problem is that there is a price involved in following it. Inspiration will take you only so far. At some point you must take charge and keep or build on the momentum. As we get our first line over to the pier at our home port, let's take a brief look at what lies behind the five key words.

1. *Mission.* What the nation expects of us and we expect of our unit and ourselves. The compass we steer by, the raison d'être of our existence, the reason we strive, work, and bleed. You must relate yourself to your command's, the Navy's, and the nation's missions and their accomplishment.

2. *People*. Missions are accomplished by people—not systems, hardware, and command structures. You nurture this resource, employ it carefully, and see that it prospers on its own terms. If your people are successful, you will be, too.

3. *Performance*. This means you get the job done—not just satisfactorily, not just well, but superbly. Professional competence and people are the keys.

4. *Command.* It is what we prepare for in the first half of our careers and what sets the stage for a successful second half.

5. *Sea*. Our unique environment. It brings the other four components together: Excellent *performance* in *command* at *sea* in pursuit of an important *mission* that is accomplished through *people* we lead.

26

Swallowing the Anchor
What Is Your Legacy to the Service?

> From first to last the seaman's thoughts are very much
> concerned with his anchors.
> —Joseph Conrad[1]

For most readers of this book retirement seems a long way off. Perhaps you are early in your career and are not even sure you will stay until retirement ("swallowing the anchor"). Or you are in mid career and if you think of retirement at all, it is about what you will do after you leave the Navy. But for the rest of you the time is fast approaching when you must "swallow the anchor" and leave the Navy behind. For the officer who tries to understand what it all means, he or she may ask: Did I make a difference? Or, what is the legacy I leave behind? Of what am I most proud in my years of service?

If you are a junior officer, many of your bosses served through the decades-long Cold War. If you are already in retirement, the chances are that most of your bosses served in World War II. Many of their bosses served in World War I. In my lifetime there was a former CNO who wrote about his experiences as a midshipman during the Civil War. The common element is a continuous chain of service to our country. This service saw arduous sea operations, particularly during World War II and the Cold War that followed. There were long deployments, years in some cases, active combat, and facing an enemy who made sure you knew what an "incoming" was. Entire new generations of ships and aircraft entered service and were replaced by even newer ones.

This recycling continues into our own day. Each summer an entire new crop of ensigns enters the service and they will measure themselves against your footsteps just as your seniors measured themselves against those of my generation. Much in the Navy has changed during the course of the past seventy years—from the parsimonious but dangerous peace of the thirties to the uncertainty and surge operations of today's fleet. We no longer look for Nazi or Soviet submarines, or land ground forces on hostile shores as during World War II or Korea. But we face today our own challenges of adapting the Navy to meet the challenge of new adversaries no more caring about human life or freedom than were their predecessors.

What will you contribute to this chain of service and renewal? A wise flag officer who is both a friend and once was my boss had a ready answer to that question. Your legacy is your junior officers, the example you set, the way you train them, the way you lead them, the way you teach them what is important and what is not, and what is enduring and what is a passing fad. A sobering thought. It is not the changes you made, the systems you helped the Navy acquire, the enemies vanquished, the ordnance you delivered on target, your retention rate, the promotions you earned, the decorations you wear, the honors you have received. It comes down to the people who are the lifeblood of today's Navy and that of the future. It is a priceless national treasure and you will, if you do your job, be a part of it.

Want some evidence? Examine the cases of the navies of the former Soviet Union and today's Peoples Republic of China. After World War II the Soviets embarked on a program to build a world-class navy largely from scratch. They put the mobilized resources of an entire continent behind the effort. They built an impressive edifice—hundreds of submarines, dozens of cruisers and destroyers all bristling with guns and missiles. At one time they had us seriously worrying about our maritime superiority. They had forces deployed all over the world, matching us theater by theater. They were confident enough to take us up to the brink of war in the Berlin Crisis of 1961, the Cuban Crisis in 1962, and the several Eastern Mediterranean crises of the early 1970s.

In spite of all this show of muscle, it was clear to acute observers of naval power that the Soviets had an important but largely hidden weakness: most of their personnel were not up to the job. Most were insufficiently educated, trained, motivated, and led to sustain a really effective blue-water navy. Their inheritance was a spotty one: a Czarist record of incompetence and mutiny, further tarnished by a Communist regime of political commissars and party hacks who nearly bled the professionalism out of the service. While they had some technical achievements (e.g., submarine quieting, missilery, nuclear power), they could not operate and maintain an effective modern Navy in the age of technological transformation. They had no legacy of victory, of service divorced from politics, and no officer procurement and training system that was up to the requirement.

Even after thirty or more years of sustained and costly investment and development they never managed to put to sea a fully capable and integrated carrier strike group with a modern carrier as its centerpiece. In the cat-and-mouse game of intelligence gathering our submarine force outsmarted and out-sailed theirs at almost every turn. Funds and industrial capacity were not the problems in the old Soviet Union; people were. The gap between the quarterdeck and the deck plates was as deep as it was in Czarist days. The only tradition on the deck plates was revolution, mistreating recruits, and sullen acceptance; the only tradition in the wardroom was political survival. The evidence is in the rusting hulks near Vladivostok and the Kola Peninsula today.

People's Republic of China may be headed down much the same track. Not that we should underestimate their determination and hard-won professional competence. There will be shiny new hardware, impressive exercises and demonstrations, saber rattling, and probably some crises to test our nerve. But the Chinese government will see that you can't just acquire an effective navy no matter how many five-year plans you patch together. It must be built ship by ship but you must start with your officer corps not party hacks and slogans. A legacy of professionalism and leadership is just as important by its absence as its presence. Political reliability is a poor substitute for professionalism and excellent skill training.

The purpose of this brief history lesson is to inform you that you are a part of a piece of serious national business and that your contribution is vital. It is your legacy that will keep the Navy the enduring strong right arm of the republic. It means that the attention you pay to the education and training of your midshipmen, officer candidates, and junior officers is the lifeblood of the service. It starts and ends with you.

There is an old saying in the Navy that goes something like this: When you leave your ship, you take something of it with you and something of yourself remains behind. When you leave the Navy, what will you leave behind as your legacy? Did you make a difference?

Appendix A
Service Selection: Advice Midshipmen Can Use

Service selection at the Naval Academy is a four-year system that empha-sizes warfare specialty familiarization, summer cruises, career information programs, and counseling by officers assigned to the Naval Academy. Cur-rently it is a two-step process in the senior year at the academy. The first major event is service assignment in the fall of the senior year, the culmi-nation of the service selection process. Then in February of the senior year midshipmen participate in "Ship and Class Date Selection" night, where specific ship assignments and class start dates are determined. The service selection process is less intensive and extensive in other commissioning programs but the principles involved are the same.

Despite this systemization there is still a large area of chance involved in the process. The biggest variable is the prospective officer him- or her-self. For the most part the midshipman or officer candidate is choosing not only a warfare specialty that in most cases lasts a professional lifetime but is also making bets on his or her future prospects of career success and promotion. Unfortunately most aspirants make these choices with insufficient knowledge of either themselves or the service specialty they plan to enter. The result is that the most important decision most officer aspirants are likely to make occurs before commissioning. To further raise the stakes the Navy is not a service that facilitates crossing from one warfare or restricted line (e.g., engineering duty) community to another with ease and without cost.

During a period of more than half a century I have seen officer aspi-rants make every conceivable mistake in selecting their warfare specialty and in many cases their first ship assignment on commissioning. Most mistakes center on misleading first impressions, a misplaced focus on home port rather than platform, the attractiveness of service career fads, and most fundamentally, a lack of awareness of their own personal capabilities and limitations. Part of this is the result of the unavoidable exuberance of youth and a focus on "now" rather than the future. Very few officer aspirants think beyond their first assignment. Even fewer look at a lifetime of service except in very vague terms.

What advice can be given to otherwise able young men and women with short time horizons and unlimited confidence in their own abilities and adaptability? Isn't it a bit much to expect these young people to think like future admirals and take a career-long view? Isn't it a little early to have young officers focus on hard work and the promotions that might result? The questions suggest the answers. But because this book is about performance, assignments, and promotions and the best advice that can be provided, I owe junior readers some guidelines through these hazardous waters—if they are trying to keep their options for the future open.

1. Select a warfare specialty that will challenge you but is within your capabilities. Take a hard look at those capabilities and convince yourself that you are up to the challenges. To be a pro takes more than desire: it takes hard work, and the mental and physical equipment to compete.

2. Be skeptical of potential fads. Some officer aspirants are drawn by the glamour of a television program (e.g., *JAG*), a movie (e.g., *Top Gun*), the news headlines of the war on terrorism (e.g., SEALs), popular books on some aspect of naval warfare, or some transient phenomenon (e.g., bonuses).

3. Do not focus on home port to the exclusion of warfare platforms and deployment cycles. Some officers are so intrigued by a particular home port (e.g., Hawaii, San Diego) that they prejudice their career for short-term preferences.

4. Do not let monetary considerations (e.g., bonuses, special pays) determine your warfare specialty.

5. Realize that there are pecking orders within individual warfare communities wherein some specialized subcommunities historically have enjoyed higher promotion rates than others.

6. Realize that some warfare specialties have subcommunities that may involve platforms of little potential interest. For example, although you may sign on for naval aviation with an eye to flying jet fighters, you may find yourself in the cockpit of a helicopter delivering supplies to forces afloat. Both missions are important but based on experience; they have profoundly different career advancement and assignment opportunities.

7. Do not focus on a cushy deployment schedule or a path that seems to promise maximum time at home or ashore. The proper place for a *sea officer* is at sea, not tied up to a pier or in a shipyard.

8. Do not listen to the crowd or go into a specialty because that is where many of your friends are going.

9. Do not go into a warfare specialty with the presumption in the back of your mind that if you don't like it you can change it.

10. Do not select a warfare specialty because the skills acquired there are readily transferred to post-service employment (e.g., the airlines, nuclear power industry, business management).

11. Realize that all warfare specialties involve hard work and there is not an easy path to success. "Fur-lined" jobs are for transients who don't intend to stick around or rise to the top of their profession.

12. Realize that going to sea is the Navy's business and that the further and longer you are away from the sea the less successful you will be unless you are planning on a career in the staff corps or restricted line.

13. One ship or air squadron is *not* the same as any other. Smaller units usually offer more responsibility earlier. It is easier to be lost in the shuffle in a larger unit. Large units include carriers, large amphibs,

tenders, patrol and reconnaissance squadrons. Small units include submarines, destroyers, carrier squadrons.

14. A ship's operating schedule is important. If you are ordered to a ship just going into the yard for overhaul or conversion, you will start behind in obtaining the necessary warfare qualifications.

15. Realize that the fleet is the *real* world. You cannot drop or audit courses, request a transfer, or shop for an easy curriculum in the fleet; you play the hand you are dealt and you muff it at your peril.

16. Treat service or warfare specialty selection as the most important early decision in your professional life. Caveat emptor.

17. Ships or squadrons that rarely or infrequently deploy overseas are the functional equivalent of shore duty. Not the place to be early in your career.

18. Select a ship or squadron type that fires weapons at the enemy. Other units are important to the Navy but not necessarily to your career progress.

19. If there is a war going on, seek orders to a unit that will play a role in it.

20. Realize that your orders may be changed by the Navy to meet the needs of the service. There is no "promise" that can't be broken if the needs of the service require it.

21. Don't mortgage your future by deciding too early that you are in only for the short term. I have seen countless officers start with that attitude and decide later, after a taste of the responsibility and adventure of active service, that they want to stay longer—even for a full career. For some it is too late and they are saddled with the effect of ill-considered earlier decisions.

22. Successful academy and college athletes are particularly vulnerable. Their sport has been such a big part of their lives that some select career options that facilitate continuing that interest with an eye to more playing time or eventually the pros or coaching. Those following this course are making a bet against very heavy odds.

Appendix B
Advice from Others

Junior officers have been receiving advice from their seniors since the beginning of warfare. This appendix contains a sampling of relevant articles applicable to today's naval officers. In addition there are several books on the subject. All are worth reading.[1] While the advice provided here reflects much of the conventional wisdom of senior officers who have had successful careers, such wisdom usually focuses more on what the junior officer should be or become rather than *how* to achieve it. Most authors provide guidelines for professional conduct but are short on details and examples. The book before the reader and its predecessor, *Career Compass*, are attempts to bridge this gap.[2]

I vividly remember seeing excellent and poor examples of leadership and performance going back to my midshipman days. As the years passed and my career unfolded I gradually perceived the close relationship between professional performance and career success: paths best taken and those to be avoided. Validate for yourself the advice you are receiving and will receive. Keep a notebook. Call it a "performance notebook," not a career notebook. A baseline for such a log or notebook might be the advice contained in this appendix and examples provided elsewhere in this book. Your observations and the distillation of the best advice will provide you with a continuing round of bearings as you navigate through the shoal water of a full career.

In the extracts and articles to follow, my personal favorite is Capt. Chris Nichols's "Ten Things You Should Know Before You Join the Fleet." Captain Nichols was not destined to make flag rank but he had an exemplar career including holding three commands. Forceful and direct, he knows what he is talking about, and you will benefit from following in his wake.

A. Niblack's Advice to His Son[3]

In the Navy, after you have been in it a certain number of years, everyone knows you, has you labeled, sized up, and catalogued. If you have gotten into trouble, it is lovingly remembered and fixed to your name. . . .

However, line officers are the only class of people who have actually and continuously had to demonstrate their fitness to hold their jobs, and the only ones who have to take a chance of being "smirched" after making good on all the requirements. Meanwhile, from year to year the great uplift movement goes on, always-new schemes to improve the efficiency of line officers, physically, mentally, and morally. Examinations become more rigid. New tests are exacted. Inspections are made to test the efficiency of commanding officers, and every year the plucking knife sinks deeper and deeper.

Meanwhile nobody else under the government has necessarily to know much of anything, except to be geographically and politically well located. There is no examination for ambassador, collector of internal revenue, postmaster-general, marshal, district attorney, interstate commerce commissioner, etc. It is merely a question of getting an appointment, and being confirmed by the Senate.

It is therefore some achievement, after all, to survive the slings and sorrows of outrageous fortune, and to retire on age for attaining age 62 as a rear admiral, U.S. Navy.

B. Wilbur's Suggestions for Navy Junior Line Officers[4]

1. Be forehanded. Read, listen, question, think ahead.
2. At each stage of your career, know your job and your equipment.

3. Use every opportunity to develop skills in seamanship and/or airmanship.

4. Learn navigation. The ocean is a very large place. Know where you are—the Global Positioning System might not be available when you need it.

5. Strive to develop leadership skills. Read. Learn from successful leaders.

6. Learn to write good Navy English. This skill is treasured by commanding officers, executive officers, and department heads.

7. Join the Naval Institute. Read and study history.

8. Find out about the Navy Mutual Aid Association. It is an organization you can trust.

9. Get as much education as you can. It will enrich your life in countless ways. The Navy encourages this, but you have to do the work.

10. Keep yourself in good physical condition. Exercise regularly.

11. Go easy on the alcohol consumption. It is a cultural hazard in the military.

12. Keep a diary. Your children will be glad you did—and so will you in later life.

13. Be optimistic. Optimists are wrong as often as pessimists, but they have happier lives.

C. Nichols's Advice to a Junior Officer Reporting to the Fleet[5]

"I wish someone would tell me the truth." It is the mantra of midshipmen from time immemorial. They seem to feel as though external forces are controlling all the information they receive, withholding some that might be vital, and feeding them other information that is extraneous. It is as though they are catching glimpses of the real world, but someone is withholding a full view.

So here is the truth from the fleet. Whether you are departing the confines of Bancroft Hall at the U.S. Naval Academy, graduating from an

NROTC program, or completing Officer Candidate School, these are the ten things you should know before you go on board your ship, enter your squadron, or join your platoon.

The Five Basic Responses

Yes, sir. No, sir. Aye aye, sir. I'll find out, sir. No excuse, sir. As plebes, midshipmen are limited to these five responses. For their remaining three years at the academy, they try to cast them off. In the fleet, you ignore them at your peril.

I could not care less for an officer who tells me, "I think so, sir," or "I told them to, sir," or "It should be, sir." Try giving those responses to questions such as, "Is that fuel tank safe to enter," or "Has the ejection seat been repaired?" "Are your spaces secured for sea?" "Is your weapon safe?"

As one three-star said to me when my ship was responsible for range clearance for a combined surface and air-launched Harpoon shot, "When you tell me the range is clear, I want that to mean within a *metaphysical certitude* that there is no one on the range. Is the range clear?"

"I think so, sir," probably would not have satisfied the metaphysical certitude criterion.

Qualifications of a Naval Officer

You memorized it because you had to. But once you are in the fleet, you will have to live by its rules, for the great truth is this: you are being watched. Not just by me, but by every Sailor and Marine in your charge. They will watch the way you dress, the way you act, the way you stand watch, the way you behave on liberty, and the way you hold yourself in front of them at morning quarters. They will take their cues from you and live according to how you live. While a classmate might be indifferent to your unpolished shoes, unkempt hair, or ill-fitting uniform, a chief, or even a seaman will not share that indifference. From a chief you will get advice delivered behind closed doors in deliberate, measured tones. From a seaman, it will be a slam-dunk, as in "I'll shine my shoes when you shine yours, *sir*."

So, yes learning the "Qualifications of a Naval Officer" is rote memorization. Yet, "Qualifications" contain definitive, unapologetic, unerring guidance on what Sailors and seniors expect of their division officers. They will not want a new friend, and they will not want you to share your tattoo with them in some misguided effort to be one of the boys. Instead, they want someone they can look up to, someone they can be proud of as you walk down the pier, someone they can respect. In a word, you should remember "the great truth, that to be well obeyed, you must be perfectly esteemed."

"The Laws of the Navy"

"The Laws of the Navy," written by Royal Navy Adm. Ronald Hopwood at the turn of the 19th century contains exceptional words to live by that offer a solid foundation on which to build your future. You cannot separate "Laws of the Navy" and "Qualifications of a Naval Officer." One without the other is incomplete. Both recognize that to be a competent officer, you will have to be "perfectly esteemed," and that you must put your Sailors' welfare ahead of your own.

Consider the whole of the "Laws" to be scripture, but here is a fleet favorite:

So live that thou bearest the strain.

When you walk on board and greet your troops for the first time, they will want to know what your standards are. They will take their cues initially from the way you carry yourself, your demeanor, and your appearance. That is only the start, however. You will be tested daily on your adherence to the standards you have set. Either you train the way you fight or you don't. It is simple as that. If you do, you will bleed less in war.

It is anathema to have occasional lapses in your standards. These lapses will be beacons in an otherwise dark night that attract attention and invite replication. You must set the standard and live it on a daily basis, because it is impossible to know when you will suffer the heat and light of crisis or war. At the academy or in college we were all taught we rated what we got away with. This attitude breeds innovation and resiliency, even if that resiliency rests in how you bounce back from a black "N" (what midshipmen receive after getting 50 demerits from infractions). In the fleet, on the other hand, you will get away with nothing less than an honest mistake. Cutting corners, taking shortcuts, or choosing the easy road—in short, not bearing the strain—will result in ships running aground, planes flying into the water, or Marines lives at risk. . . .

Your life at sea is arduous, and you will find that your temper flares as your patience diminishes. Take leave. Go home. Go kayaking. Do *something*—just get away from it all, and give your people room to grow.

You are not indispensable, and you never will achieve perfection. Give your people a chance to take charge, the opportunity to do things on their own, even while knowing you might do things differently. Striving for constant improvement is good. Striving for perfection—doing everything yourself because you are afraid someone else will not get it right—is nuts. You will drive yourself and your people insane.

The Honor Concept

Lie once, tell one half-truth, deny one transgression to your commanding officer or to your Sailors, and they will cease to see you as a person of honor. You will no longer be "perfectly esteemed," and you will be discounted and cast aside.

Here is another great truth: you will be tested daily. Your Sailors, your ship, your squadron, your plane, or your platoon will test you every day. When a chief brings you a piece of paper to sign that both you and he know is not exactly true, you are being tested. Sign it, and you fail the test. I assure you, another tainted piece of paper will be close on its heels. Read the history of the MV-22 Osprey program. Read about the operations officer who signed off on an inventory of all (well, almost all) the secret material in the safe. Or read the story of the dynamics in the control room of the (SSN-772) on 11 February 2001.

Take Nothing at Face Value

Do not take the routines of the fleet as a simple activity. They are much more than habitual chores.

It is like marching at the academy. Marching is not really about marching: it is about instant obedience to an order, performing flawlessly as a team, and publicly displaying the skill and pride resident in your company.

Three times a day underway we routinely pass "sweepers, sweepers man your brooms, give the ship a clean sweep-down fore and aft." But sweepers is more than just sweeping, and more than just cleaning the ship. Sweepers is about issuing an order, following up on it, and giving guidance when necessary and praise when warranted. It is about getting out of your stateroom and talking to your people.

It is here that you will find out that Seaman Bradley needs help finding more time to work on his college courses because he never learned how to budget his time, or that Fireman Hill's wife is pregnant and about to give birth, and he cannot get anyone below you to work on his chit. Just talking to your people can have an amazing effect. When it comes time for Sailors to check out with the commanding officer and leave the command, they vividly remember that one time "my division officer did not have time to talk to me."

Work for Yourself

You are a first classman, a senior. Now you are at the pinnacle of your academy or college career. You have all the power, all the glory, and all the freedom—or at least more than you have had for the past three years. Once you graduate and become an ensign or second lieutenant, why would you want to give up your autonomy?

Firsties at the academy pretty much work for themselves within the confines of "Mother B" (Bancroft Hall). You can have that status on your ship, in your squadron, or in your platoon if your standards are high. If you set your standards for your spaces higher than the accepted status quo, you will be able to set your own hours, prioritize your work, and work under your own direction. In short, you will work for yourself.

On the other hand, if your standards are lower than those of your boss, you always will work for him. In trying to get you to meet his standards, he will end up telling you what to do, when to do it, and how it should be done. It is unpleasant to have to grab a division officer and lead him to his unkempt auxiliary machinery room and say, "What do you intend to do about this?" I would much rather have him come to *me*, grab me by the elbow, and tell me, "Look what my Sailors have done."

Sailors will obey you because you have exercised good leadership, because you have practiced good order and discipline, because you have set an example, and because you bear the strain every day. You will earn their trust by treating them right. Then they will obey you because you have earned that right. Once you earn that trust, it becomes the most cherished of your possessions, and you will do nothing that puts it in jeopardy. . . .

Sailors do not like to be used as stepping stones. If you have not figured that out, I will tell you: you exist for them, not the other way around.

You Will Fail Occasionally; You Will Make Mistakes
I have made mistakes every step of the way to being a captain in command, and I continue to make them. You, too, will make mistakes—but knowing that you tried, that you were not malicious, that you were willing to be "the man in the arena," all these will make the difference. True leaders can discern "error from malice, thoughtlessness from incompetence, and well meant shortcoming from heedless or stupid blunder," so your chief or your bluejackets or your department head or your commanding officer will pick you up, dust you off, and tell you to

go try again. I do not give a damn for anyone who is afraid to get into the arena and make a mistake. You learn from your mistakes, and your people learn from theirs.

There is an accommodation ladder from the USS *Sumter* (LST-1181) at the bottom of the basin in Little Creek, Virginia. I put it there as a junior officer.

Have Fun

At the Naval Academy, midshipmen are restricted and held back. And yet, through it all, they learn how to have fun. Being in the Navy, as arduous as it is, is about having fun. It is adventure, exhilaration, heartache, and worth, all wrapped up in a single package. You are supposed to have fun, and you are supposed to be seen having fun. I do not care for martyrs—those who are forever going about saying, "Woe is me! See how hard I work, and how dedicated I am." It's boring. I want you to have fun, even after you have screwed up.

Let me say it again: being in the Navy is about having fun. Personally, I have had a blast. My junior officers who have taken oil smugglers over the horizon have had fun. Earning the respect and admiration of your division is fun. Port visits are fun. The wardroom is fun. The train to Tokyo, the tram to Corcovado, the roads to Rome, and the footpath up Mount Fuji are all fun. Fort Lauderdale, Coronado, San Diego, Newport, and Virginia Beach are fun. Life is a hoot beyond the breakwater. Go there.

Remember Your School and Classmates

It is an odd thing. Twenty years from now, you will live your life in the fervent hope that you will not do something that embarrasses your school or your classmates. It helps to keep things in perspective. Be true to your school.

The Elements of Style *by William Strunk Jr. and E. B. White*
Get a copy and read it.

You wanted the truth; there it is. You get a clean slate in the fleet—nobody cares that you have three black Ns or that you were the brigade commander or the captain of the football team. We care only that you perform, put ship and shipmates first, try hard, and speak the truth. So much of what you did in school is immediately, unconditionally, and irrevocably transferable to the fleet. Not by happenstance, but by design. We in the fleet want what they have been giving you the past four years. It is the real world.

See you in the fleet.

D. Kacher's Advice for a Junior Officer Just Reporting Aboard[6]

As migratory as the private sector has become, few professions outside the military average ten or more new starts in a 20-year period. Service members play the role of new guy more times than we care to remember. (In today's Navy, *new guy* refers to both men and women.) Nearly every wardroom, chief's mess, and division has stories or traditions that focus on the new arrivals to the command. Over the past decade, the Navy has emphasized that the new guy is not someone to nickname or needle, but a new teammate to lead. Mentor programs, well-orchestrated check-in procedures, and strong training systems have been designed to help arrivals new to commands.

The process of building new naval leaders is a partnership between the command and the new guy. While leaders should make sure their new guy has the opportunity to succeed, there are things you—as the new guy—can do to accelerate your learning curve. These suggestions will never substitute for hard work and a warrior ethic, but they address some of the successes and pitfalls experienced in the first commands of the numerous people who have gone before you. While many of these tips are tailored to new ensigns reporting to their first ships, most are universal and should help anyone who is new to the Navy-Marine Corps community.

1. *Write it down.* Whether you are a division officer or a petty officer, the tasking you receive in the service is often far more complex than what you experienced in civilian life, and forgetting a task affects many more people than yourself. Life is too busy and your shipmates' dependence on you is too great for you not to write down taskings.

2. *Read the instructions.* Reading the instructions and knowing the rules go a long way to ensuring success. As you manage programs such as hearing protection or heat stress that guard your Sailors' health, or plan for a missile shoot, you will benefit from finding out what the reference directs. It will be one of the first questions a good boss will ask you when he or she reviews your plan or program.

3. *Remember that respect and humility go a long way.* One of the key ingredients in today's Navy is respect regardless of rank. Knowledge, expertise, and talent are not always commensurate with rank. When Sailors, chiefs, or department heads sense you are serious about what you are learning and whom you are learning from, they will be eager to share their knowledge with you.

4. *Focus on your Sailors.* Although you are new, one job that starts right away is your duty to properly manage and care for those in your division. You will not be able to approve every request chit that crosses your desk, but it is your job to take care of your Sailors so they can take care of the mission. Everything from pay to professional development is part of your portfolio as a division officer—or as a work center supervisor. Learn each Sailor's face, rank, and last name, along with his or her family situation and goals.

5. *Gauge your command's problem-solving culture.* Every ship or squadron is a little different. Some use briefings and "chalk talks" to hash out issues and differences, while others expect that all but the most emergent issues will be arranged ahead of the final brief.

While no command ever wants a question to go unasked that will improve performance or ensure safety, your command may expect most of the details to be resolved prior to, and outside the briefing room. Well ahead of time ask mentors or bosses for their views of the expectations for the tasks at hand.

6. *Look for multiple mentors.* Your ship will assign a mentor to you, but you never have too many mentors at your disposal. New ensigns' predecessors, the officers they work for, their chiefs, and their command master chiefs, among others play mentoring roles. Good leaders, who may see things from different levels, will provide a more complete perspective than just one adviser.

7. *Seek professional training opportunities.* Most commands will have a number of formal training opportunities as you begin your training on board, and informal opportunities will abound that can help you improve your professional competency. An extra hour on the bridge, in the engineering plant, in the combat information center, or on a duty night with the right mentor could equal an entire day's learning elsewhere.

8. *Ask how you can help.* Dell CEO Michael Dell once remarked that the person who asks, "How can I help?" versus, "How do I get promoted?" always has a place in his organization. The same goes for those reporting to their first commands. Whether it is calling out ranges during an underway replenishment detail, or helping to proofread a memo, looking for ways to make a contribution will quickly make you part of the team.

9. *Build professional friendships off the ship.* Make an effort to get to know peers from other commands. Having friends outside the ship's lifelines will allow you to trade best practices and perspectives differently from how you might with shipmates from your new command. The officers, chiefs, and petty officers with strong peer relationships outside the lifelines often are the best problem solvers in a pinch.

10. *Phrases to watch out for.* The vast majority of the people you will
    serve with in the Navy and Marine Corps will be tremendous
    professionals, but even the best organizations can slip into com-
    placency. Here are some phrases to look out for: "It's always been
    that way." Don't bet on it—if something does not look like it has
    been done properly, it probably has not. "We don't really have a
    written plan. We just make it happen." With Sailors and Marines
    routinely performing complex and potentially dangerous tasks,
    few evolutions occur without being well planned. "Most of our
    training is on the job." Some of the most exciting and rewarding
    training you will do may happen on the job; however, the best
    training plans combine instruction with on-the-job training
    opportunities. Whether the trainee is you or your newest Sailor,
    make sure training is deliberate and well thought out.
11. *Allow plenty of time.* From the first day of boot camp or officer's
    training we learn that punctuality is next to godliness in the Navy
    and Marine Corps. The lesser-known corollary is that almost every
    task or challenge will take longer than you think. Make a habit of
    early arrivals and preparation.
12. *Run a good meeting.* Even as the new person, you will quickly find
    yourself running, or at the very least, significantly participating in,
    numerous meetings. One of them, divisional quarters, will afford
    you an opportunity to address your troops from the first day you
    assume duties as a division officer. Never take for granted this
    opportunity to communicate with your Sailors. For more tradi-
    tional meetings, simple things like an agenda promulgated ahead
    of time, letting participants know what is expected of them ahead
    of time, and pre-established goals make meetings count. If you do
    not think you can drive this process, ask your department head or
    chief for help. Once the meeting is complete, send out a memo or
    e-mail to ensure everyone understands what has been decided and
    what follow-up actions are required.

13. *Practice, practice, practice.* Dry runs save lives. Briefs for special evolutions that are your division's primary responsibility may be the first "public" briefing to fall on your shoulders, so make this opportunity count. One way is to rehearse your presentation, preferably with your department head or a mentor who is a particularly good briefer. Remember the brief is not the end product, but the start of a process that should include safety briefs, rehearsals, and training before your team performs its duties at full speed.

14. *Be yourself.* Demonstrate the positive qualities that ensured your success before entering the Navy. Hard work, brains, and a desire to succeed will never go out of style on our ships, squadrons, and submarines. Strategically approaching your role as the new arrival will allow you to quickly use your talents to better serve the command, your division, and yourself.

15. *Remember you are committed to a higher calling.* Although most of these pointers might apply to managing a successful debut in any type of organization, never forget the bottom line of our "business" is the national defense. Take your profession seriously—your Sailors, Marines, and the nation deserve it.

E. Olson's Rules[7]

As officers you will hold different jobs from the enlisted force. Your position is not about rank and power, it is about responsibility and accountability. Use your authority to lead, manage, champion, and nurture the force.

You are not expected to know everything, but you are expected to work and to lead at the upper levels of your knowledge, skill, and authority.

1. Know your mission, roles, and duties; understand the intent and priorities of your boss, and remember that you work for him.

2. Be a teammate. What is good for the team has priority over what is good for you.

3. Demonstrate professionalism in all that you do. Be sharp, look sharp.

4. Learn the capabilities and limitations of your people and equipment; acknowledge that the prime measure of your performance is their performance.

5. Realize that your people are very sharp, motivated, aware, and skilled; teach, coach, guide, and mentor your force, but don't claim expertise that you don't have.

6. Avoid a "zero defect" mentality, but remember that breaches of integrity and malicious violations are not "mistakes." Treat them seriously.

7. Never sacrifice what you know is right for what is convenient or expedient.

8. Be a careful steward of resources in order to get maximum value from every dollar or man hour. You have a responsibility to manage effectively but in the crunch between efficiency and effectiveness, go for effectiveness every time.

9. Train hard with realism. Practice failure so you will know how to deal with it.

10. Treat safety as a mission imperative and everybody's responsibility. Be willing to accept necessary risk, but never put the mission of your force at risk unnecessarily.

11. Communicate up, down, and across the force to build maximum situational awareness for leaders at every level. Remember that a signal or a message is not communicated until it is acknowledged.

12. Live the life of a leader—one of values, character, courage, and discipline. Use your time off constructively doing things that make you or others better in some way.

13. Realize that what you do and what you tolerate in your presence demonstrate your standards far more than what you say.

14. Empower your subordinate leaders at every level to work at the full level of their authority. Cause them to take full responsibility for their leadership decisions. Train them, trust them, and hold them to standard.

15. Wherever there are two or more of you, one of you is in charge.

16. Learn to manage your time and the time of your subordinates. Give your subordinates as much predictability in their private lives as you can. Don't waste their time.

17. Understand that life is not a popularity contest. You don't have to be liked to be effective, but you do have to be respected.

18. Be open, honest, and accurate in all your communications. Never withhold bad news from your boss.

19. Above all, remember that you serve the nation in a most demanding and most honorable profession. Treat every day in the Navy as an opportunity and a privilege.

Appendix C
The Navy Family

To today's midshipmen and junior officers a serious discussion of the role the Navy family plays in a successful career may seem to be a "stretch." But senior officers know better. The service has come a very long way indeed from the old bromide, "If they wanted you to have one, they would have issued you one [a spouse]." True, in most cases family members do not go to general quarters or man aircraft but they provide necessary support to those who do.[1]

I know of no greater change in Navy life over the past fifty years than the increased importance of family ties and support for our warriors. The Navy's leadership takes the family's role very seriously because it recognizes that a Sailor worried about his or her family is not likely to be a fully effective one. Effective Sailors win battles.

During the wars of the twentieth century the leadership of the armed services was often confounded by unacceptable absent without leave rates and the low morale associated with long deployments (often years). These developments could in large measure be traced back to a warrior's concern for his family's welfare back home. Add to this that the communications environment in those days (largely U.S. postal service mail) was characterized by sporadic and delayed delivery. There were few if any organized, command-sanctioned efforts to keep family members informed and almost no external support for the family other than "Navy Relief" and the American Red Cross—and their valiant efforts were often spotty, late, and underfunded. Sailors and their families were often left on their own to solve the problems associated with long deployments, low pay, and absence of suitable housing.

While there will probably always be problems in all this, the situation is manyfold better than in the years I remember as a junior officer. We now have leaders concerned about "ops tempo and pers tempo" (how long is a Sailor away from his or her home port?) and communicating to families whose sponsors are deployed (is there an e-mail connection up and operating?). Ombudsmen see to it that families' concerns are known to commanding officers. There are now family service centers, better pay, better housing, and more medical care options. Commanding officers have no difficulty in relating an effective Sailor to a satisfied if not entirely happy family. The Navy culture has changed to reflect the realities of two-career families (often two demanding careers—some where both partners are in the service), uncertain deployment schedules, single parents, and expanding family health needs and expectations.

But this book is about naval professionalism. What is the connection between family and your calling, and what should you as a professional know about it? It is safe to say that the most important decisions you will make in your life involve family: selecting a spouse, having children, advancing their welfare (e.g., providing for their education and health care), and folding family considerations into the decision to stay for a career—or not. A supportive family is just as important for a successful naval career as is dealing with Sailors and becoming a pro. What follows is not so much advice as giving you some channel markers as you consider this subject during your naval career.

1. *A family choice is also a major career choice,* and the reverse has the same implications. Some partners will have no interest in your naval career, others will take it as part of the playing field, and still others will treasure the experience (if somewhat after the fact!). If you are already convinced that a naval career is for you, bear in mind that there are other votes out there waiting to be counted. Moreover, fate can take a hand: if you have children they may develop needs (e.g., health care) that are often incompatible with a life of sea service.

A family reunion at the conclusion of an overseas deployment. The family is an integral part of a naval professional's life. Among the rites of passage are leaving on and returning from deployment, the awarding of decorations, changing station orders, taking command, and eventually retiring after a career of honorable service.

U.S. Naval Institute Photo Archives

2. *Your partner or spouse is a key factor in determining your success as a professional.* Most professional concerns are best left on board your unit. Your family is not and should not be privy to all of your workplace decisions and actions. But on career decisions (e.g., to go for a specific set of orders, an advanced degree) you are true partners. You both consider your careers, you do it together, weigh the benefits and costs of each decision, formulate the options and consequences, and vow to live by your joint decisions and their results. This reality should be faced up front. You are a team not

only in the marital sense but also in the naval sense. Some old-fashioned professionals believe they can tuck their professional and family lives into separate compartments; in today's service they are learning differently.

3. *Hardships are part of naval service.* The trick is to anticipate, understand, and overcome them as part of a family. This involves understanding that active service involves deployments, each partner having to fend for him or herself for extended periods, having to deal with uncertainty and plans changed on the fly. Those with an inflexible turn of mind will not succeed as a naval professional or as a member of a successful naval family.

4. *The intangible benefits of naval service are important, not only for the professional but also for family members.* Naval service is not about pay, prestige, and the individual. The professional's family—spouse and children—should be made a part of the equation. They are serving, too—and deserve the credit and a part in the key decisions. A professional ensures that his or her family knows what the payoff of service is to our country and nurtures the same type of teamwork that is involved in a successful division, department, or unit.

5. *There is a major social component to service life.* This is not trivial and is not to be considered as a form of "partying" (though there is some that we all enjoy). Rather, because we serve together and may die together we expect and are expected to bond to our shipmates and service friends. Part of this bonding involves social activities. If we are bonded to one another, we are more effective as a unit and as a service. A spouse who responds positively to this element of service life is a treasure and soon his or her reputation (for good or ill) and that of the uniformed partner are established. I find few sights more inspiring than to see an old pro Navy couple entertaining their junior officers and their spouses and friends with mutual warmth and affection.

6. *Don't forget the children.* Your children are (often more than we like) a reflection of how we discharge our responsibilities to service and family. Your children are not just another set of recruits. They are junior partners in your family and service joint enterprise. They deserve to be consulted—and even heeded as the realities permit. This takes some time, nurturing, patience, and only rare use of peremptory decrees from the quarterdeck.

I have known very few successful naval officers who did not also have a loving and supportive spouse and family. Some have overcome shortcomings in their family lives but in most cases known to me it has entailed a price in both personal happiness and professional effectiveness. A final piece of advice. Consider your family and your professional service as inextricably intertwined. They are separate strands but they individually only have strength when they are bonded together and tied to common objectives. The days are long gone when the Navy family was a stand-alone entity of little interest to the service command structure and the dependent variable in force deployment and resource decisions. But you as the serving member have special responsibilities to ensure that the line holds and that each strand can bear the load.

Appendix D
Professional Reading

In *Career Compass* I outlined what a junior officer's professional library might look like. That "starter set" could carry an officer through an entire career. My point was and is that the naval professional cannot rely solely on schools to become educated and proficient in the profession. There must be continued growth that is fostered through a well-thought-out reading program, a program that goes beyond the basic references of the profession.

A minimum might start and end with a close reading of the Naval Institute's *Proceedings*. Don't limit your reading to the articles that deal with your warfare specialties or special interests. Branch further afield and try reading each issue cover to cover. Sometimes this is not an easy exercise because some of the articles are very specialized or specific to another service of little immediate interest to you.

Building on that start go on to the *Naval War College Review* and *The Joint Forces Quarterly*. Unfortunately, both have limited distribution lists and you will have to exert yourself to inform their sponsors that you are a serious student of naval and joint warfare. *Navy Times* will give you the news but is often unsatisfying because of the limitations of any newspaper or weekly. Most official Navy press releases (they are available on the Internet) are often stilted, seem canned, and sometimes outdated by information received by other means. There are an enormous number of Navy home pages and Web sites available. Those sponsored by the Naval Personnel Command are particularly useful to the officer interested in how Navy personnel are being assigned, schooled, and evaluated.

Then there are the stalwarts of the naval professional literature authored in previous years by such greats as Vice Adm. Bill Mack (*The Naval Officer's Guide*) and Vice Adm. James Calvert (e.g., *The Naval Profession*) and now by Vice Adm. James Stavridis (e.g., *Division Officer's Guide*) and Lt. Cdr. Tom Cutler (e.g., *Bluejacket's Manual*). My other favorites include the writings of Capt. Wayne Hughes (e.g., *Fleet Tactics and Coastal Combat*).

Good biography is also a fertile field for your professional reading. I have in mind my particular favorite, Tom Buell's *Master of Sea Power*, a biography of Fleet Adm. Ernest J. King. But Ned Potter's biographies of admirals Nimitz, Halsey, and Burke are well worth reading. Many of the CNOs of the twentieth century have biographies (and some autobiographies). Most are revealing as to the burdens and opportunities of naval command.

As good and as necessary as these reference works are in providing a framework for understanding our profession, they do not always breathe excitement into what naval professionals sense and do in their day-to-day duties as well as in combat. In my opinion we still do not have the definitive work to guide or inform a naval combat leader today.

To fill the gap in part we have to turn to fiction and turn back two centuries for what C. S. Forester and Patrick O'Brian have done for the Royal Navy during the Napoleonic Wars. I know of no authors who so precisely capture the mood of a warship and her crew in or entering imminent combat as these two old pros. If you want to know and feel how the character of a commanding officer is transmitted to a crew and thus set the tone of the ship, read the works of these two. Neither served as a naval officer but they capture the essence of command—its successes and failures—in a dramatic narrative flow.

I have found that, in the hands of a superb author, naval fiction can be a valuable integrating device for taking the concrete facts and fashioning an understandable linkage to enduring realities and verities. A naval combat leadership course could be built around the Forester and

O'Brian naval novels. Other naval novels of particular use are Richard McKenna's *Sand Pebbles* (relating a Sailor's view to big-picture realities), Marcus Goodrich's *Delilah* (for a better understanding of the link between the mess decks and the wardroom), and Herman Wouk's *Caine Mutiny* (for understanding the corrosive effects of an eccentric skipper and an unsupportive wardroom). If you read the works of fiction I have discussed here, I will guarantee that you will have a better and deeper understanding of what underpins our profession.

Your professional reading should not stop at the borders of naval literature. You need to stretch your mind (see chapter 15) into unfamiliar territory. You might start with a good business school journal to see what is going on at the cutting edge of innovation in resource management. You could read the occasional copy of *The Chronicle of Higher Education* for a better understanding of how our brightest youth are being educated and about the latest innovations (and fads) in learning techniques. Much of the naval officer's business involves teaching and you can't be too good at it. There are many other avenues to explore. For example, look at the complete selection of periodicals handled by world-class book stores.

Then there are the history books. Take a particular interest at the interface between political and military decision making. Churchill's massive tome on the conduct of World War II (*The Second World War*) is a must-read in this genre. You will benefit from a better understanding of what political leaders expect from their military leaders and what military leaders need from their civilian leaders in wartime. As you become more senior in the service (and certainly if you reach flag rank) this interface will be of crucial importance to you and your country.

Notes

Chapter 1. What Is Expected of You?
1. Capt. Ronald Hopwood, RN, "The Laws of the Navy." Quoted in Leland P. Lovette, *Naval Customs: Traditions and Usage* (Annapolis, Md.: Naval Institute Press, 1939), 382.
2. For an excellent article that parallels the advice given here see Capt. Christopher Nichols, USN, "Ten Things You Should Know Before You Join the Fleet," U.S. Naval Institute *Proceedings* (October 2003): 96–98. For the reader's convenience it is reproduced in appendix B.

Chapter 2. Leading Sailors
1. Joseph Conrad, *A Personal Record and a Mirror of the Sea* (London: Penguin, 1998), 158.
2. *Ship's Organization and Personnel* (Annapolis, Md.: Naval Institute Press, 1972), 27.
3. See Rear Adm. James G. Stavridis, USN, and Cdr. Robert Girrier, USN, *Division Officer's Guide*, 11th ed. (Annapolis, Md.: Naval Institute Press, 2004). This book is the definitive treatment of the division officer's duties.
4. For an additional source of good advice on how to conduct yourself on reporting aboard your first duty station see Lt. Cdr. Fred W. Kacher, USN, "New Guy 101: Your First Tour of Duty," U.S. Naval Institute *Proceedings* (June 2004): 72–73. Reprinted in appendix B.
5. Terrence Robertson, *Escort Commander: Captain Frederic John Walker, The Man Who Helped Free the Atlantic of the U-Boat Menace* (1956; repr., New York: Nelson Doubleday, 1979), 75.
6. Conrad, *A Personal Record*, 194.

Chapter 3. Operational Performance
1. Conrad, *A Personal Record*, 155.

Chapter 4. Performance in the Schoolhouse

1. James A. Winnefeld Sr., *Career Compass* (Annapolis, Md.: Naval Institute Press, 2005), 53–60.
2. Some observers note that there is no downside to investing your time and effort in obtaining a postgraduate education. For example, see Lt. Col. Patrick J. Donahoe, U.S. Army, in "Naval Culture and Military Education," U.S. Naval Institute *Proceedings* (July 2005): 50–53. Some observers from the other services or academe (or both) lose sight of the many things a naval officer must do to become proficient at sea before assuming command there. The path to command in the Navy provides less time for academic study than the career patterns of the other services. Critics of Navy practice might better examine the Navy's focus on command and the necessity for frequent sea tours rather than the lack of time its future leaders spend in an academic setting. Contrary to the implications drawn by Colonel Donahoe and other critics the Navy's leadership does not have a bias *against* higher education; it has a bias *for* most valuing its officers that have held command at sea.
3. See Cdr. Clay Harris, USN, "All Detailing Is Retail," U.S. Naval Institute *Proceedings* (July 2003): 62.

Chapter 5. Transition from Junior to Senior Officer

1. Winnefeld, *Career Compass*, 165–66.

Chapter 6. Performance as a Department Head or Staff Officer

1. Hopwood, quoted in Lovette, *Naval Customs*, 381.
2. Aviators are more likely to serve in a billet in an aircraft carrier on the way to or from a squadron department head tour. These shipboard tours are most often in the air and operations departments, though a fortunate and able few serve as assistant navigator of a carrier.

Chapter 8. You and Your Detailer

1. Hilaire Belloc, quoted in James Reynolds, *Sovereign Britain* (New York: Putnam, 1955), 39.
2. Winnefeld, *Career Compass*, 109–26.
3. The "pack" is a term used by personnel managers (and increasingly in

the fleet) to describe the vast majority of officers in the middle part of
the bell-shaped performance curve. Thus a "packer" is an officer who
does not "break out" above or below most of his or her contemporaries
in performance rankings. On the other hand officers in the pack are
what makes the Navy run, even though few will be represented in its
upper leadership echelons in the future. An obvious point that many
overlook is that some 49 percent of the Navy's officers are below average
on a *comparative* ranking basis.

4. This is not to say that there is some master template that defines an ideal
career. But there are certain steps that most successful line officers hit on
the way up (e.g., command at sea in the grade of commander, key shore
billets in Washington or other major headquarters staffs).

Chapter 9. Performance in an Overseas Tour

1. Communication from Cdr. Clay Harris, USN (a former detailer).
2. Winnefeld, *Career Compass*, 91, 141, 162.

Chapter 10. Joint and Combined Duty

1. Capt. John V. Noel, USN (Ret.), and Capt. Edward L. Beach, USN (Ret.),
Naval Terms Dictionary, 5th ed. (Annapolis, Md.: Naval Institute Press,
1988), 69, 158.

Chapter 11. Serving as Executive Officer

1. The reference work for the duties of the executive officer is the *Standard
Organization and Regulations for the United States Navy*, OPNAVINST
3120.32C (SORN). See in particular pages 65–76.
2. This practice was necessary during air combat operations in World War
II when skippers were at almost as much risk as their most junior pilots.
It was necessary to have a trained replacement on board. In some cases
both the CO and XO were lost and a department head had to take over
the unit temporarily.
3. Capt. James Stavridis, USN, and Vice Adm. William Mack, USN (Ret.),
Command at Sea, 5th ed. (Annapolis, Md.: Naval Institute Press, 1998),
3. This is the skipper's bible for command at sea and combines the
efforts and experience of two old pros in the business.
4. Communication from Capt. Chris Nichols, USN.

Chapter 14. Social Polish

1. Quoted in the annual handbook of the Brigade of Midshipmen, *Reef Points*, most recently in the 100th edition (Annapolis, Md.: U.S. Naval Institute, 2005), 82.
2. Winnefeld, *Career Compass*, 99–104.

Chapter 15. Are You Still Learning?

1. Hilaire Belloc, *The Path to Rome* (Chicago: Henry Regnery Co., 1954), 57.
2. A trick that has pulled me out of a potentially tight spot. As a senior officer you will be invited to attend some official or service social functions. Many times and with little notice you will be asked to say a "few words." Anticipate this possibility and have your thoughts in order before you enter the room. The ability to anticipate the event and think quickly on your feet are virtues you should cultivate.
3. Winnefeld, *Career Compass*, 175–77.

Chapter 16. What Is Your Competitive Edge?

1. Capt. A. P. Niblack, quoted in Lovette, *Naval Customs*, xiv.

Chapter 17. Opportunities, Disappointments, and Injustices

1. Van Wyck Brooks, *The Flowering of New England, 1815–1865* (1936; repr., New York: Modern Library, 1941), 422.

Chapter 18. Your Command Tour

1. Capt. Harley F. Cope, quoted in Stavridis and Mack, *Command at Sea*, xii. Quote is from the preface to the first edition of *Command at Sea*, which Cope authored.
2. A good example is Stavridis and Mack, *Command at Sea*.
3. See Cdr. Clay Harris, USN, "All Detailing Is Retail," U.S. Naval Institute *Proceedings* (July 2003): 62.

Chapter 19. On the Waterfront

1. Capt. A. P. Niblack, quoted in Lovette, *Naval Customs*, xiv.

Chapter 21. Observing (and Learning from) Admirals at Close Range

1. Capt. Ronald Hopwood, "The Laws of the Navy." Quoted in Lovette, *Naval Customs*, 380.

2. Noted historian Barbara Tuchman made this key point. See her lecture on "Generalship," delivered at the Army War College in April 1972 and reproduced in her *Selected Essays on Practicing History* (New York: Ballantine Books, 1981), 277–79.

3. A favorite (and in my view overdone) conflict in film and television entertainment pits a senior who is single-mindedly mission oriented (if not deranged) who seems to care little for the welfare of his or her subordinates (*Twelve O'Clock High, Mr. Roberts, Caine Mutiny, The Lost Battalion*, etc.) against a subordinate who puts his or her people first. This glib portrayal makes for good drama and entertainment but betrays a singular misunderstanding of the military ethic: people and their survival make the mission possible but the mission is the top priority. If people and their survival were the top priority, we would not need the military to protect the many or to sacrifice the relatively few for the welfare of the whole.

Chapter 22. Combat: Will You Measure Up?

1. Carl LaVO, *Slade Cutter: Submarine Warrior* (Annapolis, Md.: Naval Institute Press, 2003), 246. Emphasis added. Note the roles of training, unit cohesion, and professionalism. Captain Cutter won four Navy Crosses while in command during successful submarine patrols during World War II.

2. For a gripping description of the effects of stress and fatigue in combat see Capt. William J. Ruhe, USN (Ret.), *War in the Boats: My WWII Submarine Battles* (Washington, D.C.: Brassey's, 1994), 235–65.

3. Robertson, *Escort Commander*, 73. Captain Walker was perhaps the most proficient and aggressive U-boat fighter in the Royal Navy during World War II. He was passed over for promotion in the prewar Royal Navy. He was eventually promoted to captain during the war. C. S. Forester in his novel *The Good Shepherd* draws a similar portrait of a U.S. convoy escort commander in World War II.

4. John Buchan, *Greenmantle* (1916; repr., London: Penguin Books, 1956), 241.

Chapter 23. The Intangibles of the Naval Profession

1. *Reef Points.*

Chapter 25. Perspectives of a Naval Career

1. E. M. Forster, *Howard's End* (New York: Vintage Books, 1921), 107.

Chapter 26. Swallowing the Anchor: What Is Your Legacy to the Service?

1. Conrad, *A Personal Record,* 147.

Appendix B. Advice from Others

1. See in particular Rear Adm. Rafael Benitez's *Anchors and Practical Maxims* (Annapolis, Md.: Annapolis Publishing Co., n.d.), and Vice Adm. James Calvert's *The Naval Profession* (New York: McGraw Hill, 1965).
2. Winnefeld, *Career Compass.*
3. Niblack, quoted in Lovette, xiv.
4. Harley D. Wilbur, USN (Ret.), "Wilbur's Suggestions for Navy Junior Line Officers," U.S. Naval Institute *Proceedings* (August 2004): 80.
5. Capt. Christopher Nichols, USN, "Ten Things You Should Know Before You Join the Fleet," U.S. Naval Institute *Proceedings* (October 2003): 96–98.
6. Kacher, "New Guy 101." At the time this article was written, Kacher was the executive officer for the USS *Barry* (DDG 52).
7. Taken from Dick Ardafany's "Olson's Rules," *Shipmate* (March 2005): 142. Rear Adm. Erik Olson is a reserve officer with a special operations background.

Appendix C. The Navy Family

1. I highly recommend that midshipmen and junior officers and their intended spouses read two excellent books on Navy families. The first is Laura Hall Stavridis's *Navy Spouses Guide* (Annapolis, Md.: Naval Institute Press, 2002). She is the daughter and wife of naval officers and knows her subject well. Second, I recommend Jacey Eckert's humorous (but with a message) *The Homefront Club: The Hardheaded Woman's Guide to Raising a Military Family* (Annapolis, Md.: Naval Institute Press, 2005).

Index

Page numbers in italics refer to a photograph on that page.
Page numbers followed by the letter n, *plus a number, refer to endnote text.*

About the Author

Rear Adm. James A. Winnefeld Sr. graduated from the Naval Academy in 1951. He has served in destroyers, aircraft carriers and their embarked squadrons, and amphibious ships. After four commands at sea, both in aviation and surface warfare units, he served as Commandant of Midshipmen. His early knowledge of the Navy's performance rating, promotion, and assignment systems was gained in three tours in the Bureau of Naval Personnel and in seeing those systems work (or not) from the deck plates. He served on a wide variety of personnel selection boards.

After his retirement from the Navy he was a program director for RAND, a policy analysis "think tank" for the government. While at RAND he conducted strategy and personnel management studies for the services, the combatant commands, the Department of State, the Director of Central Intelligence, and the White House. Over the years since his retirement he has maintained close ties with many former and current midshipmen. Their aspirations and questions about a naval career prompted the writing of this book and its predecessor, *Career Compass* (Naval Institute Press, 2005).

Admiral Winnefeld is the son, nephew, brother, cousin, and father of Navy men who served afloat in peace and war. He has a deep affection and respect for the Navy and its men and women.

The Naval Institute Press is the book-publishing arm of the U.S. Naval Institute, a private, nonprofit, membership society for sea service professionals and others who share an interest in naval and maritime affairs. Established in 1873 at the U.S. Naval Academy in Annapolis, Maryland, where its offices remain today, the Naval Institute has members worldwide.

Members of the Naval Institute support the education programs of the society and receive the influential monthly magazine *Proceedings* and discounts on fine nautical prints and on ship and aircraft photos. They also have access to the transcripts of the Institute's Oral History Program and get discounted admission to any of the Institute-sponsored seminars offered around the country. Discounts are also available to the colorful bimonthly magazine *Naval History*.

The Naval Institute's book-publishing program, begun in 1898 with basic guides to naval practices, has broadened its scope to include books of more general interest. Now the Naval Institute Press publishes about seventy titles each year, ranging from how-to books on boating and navigation to battle histories, biographies, ship and aircraft guides, and novels. Institute members receive significant discounts on the Press's more than eight hundred books in print.

Full-time students are eligible for special half-price membership rates. Life memberships are also available.

For a free catalog describing Naval Institute Press books currently available, and for further information about joining the U.S. Naval Institute, please write to:

Customer Service

U.S. Naval Institute

291 Wood Road

Annapolis, MD 21402-5034

Telephone: (800) 233-8764

Fax: (410) 571-1703

Web address: www.navalinstitute.org